IMORTALON

BY THE SAME AUTHOR

FICTION
The Village Buyers
L*S*I*T*T (in softcover: Takeover)
The Craving
Aries Rising
Glad to Be Here
IQ 83
Orca
Heat
Earthsound
The Swarm

NONFICTION

How to Write Almost Anything Better and Faster
Seventeen Days: The Katie Beers Story
The Woodchipper Murder
Vesco: From Wall Street to Castro's Cuba
The B.S. Factor
McCarthy for President
The Church Trap
The War/Peace Establishment

IMORTALON

ARTHUR HERZOG

iUniverse Star
New York Lincoln Shanghai

IMORTALON

iUniverse Star
an iUniverse, Inc. imprint

For information address:
iUniverse, Inc.
2021 Pine Lake Road, Suite 100
Lincoln, NE 68512
www.iuniverse.com

ISBN: 0-595-29762-5

Printed in the United States of America

Thanks to my advisers:

Robert B. Brooks, Ph.D.

Joseph Sacco, M.D.

Anna Jakubowaka, M.D., M.B.A..

Clinical Drug Development

Poulenc Rorer

Marian Kruszynski, Ph.D., D.Sc.

Research Scientist, Centocor

Lourdes C. Felarca, M.D.

Associate Medical Director, Pfizer

A gene that confers fountain-of-youth properties on human cells grown in laboratory glassware has been tested in mice to see if its absence will cause the opposite effect, that of premature aging. The answer—which is partly yes—sustains but does not yet fulfill the hope that manipulations of the gene will provide treatments for cancer, heart disease and other maladies of aging human tissues.

—The New York Times, March 5, 1999

....most of the scientists at the meeting (on postponed aging) said, the question no longer is "Will it happen?" but rather "When?" "There's nothing bigger," Dr. Steven Austad said. "If we could do it, there's nothing bigger. It's the big enchilada."

—The New York Times, March 9, 1999

An anti-aging pill could be the ultimate blockbuster drug. People, particularly aging baby boomers, already spend billions of dollars to fight the ravages of aging with medicines and procedures. But those solutions tackle one problem at a time. At least in theory, an anti-aging pill could postpone the onset of many problems simultaneously. Such a pill could be taken not only by people with a certain disease but potentially by everyone.

—The New York Times, September 21, 2003

We all labour against our own cure,
for death is the cure of all diseases.

—Sir Thomas Browne

PROLOGUE

▼

Strange how little things can upset you, Freddie thought, as the mirror told her she had a tiny furrow between her eyes that hadn't been there the night before. A stanza from Adelaide Crapsey's "On Seeing Weather-beaten Trees" flashed into her mind.

> "Is it as plainly in our living shown,
> By slant and twist, which way the wind hath blown?"

Well, which? Aging, of course, in her case premature aging, no small matter. Could stress be responsible? She'd had plenty of that, the reason she'd stayed cooped up in her mansion, reading poetry to calm her nerves. Would the new drug her company had produced make people live much longer? Almost forever? What were the implications of that? Would oldsters rule the world? If individuals lived for centuries, they probably would.

Only one human had taken the capsules and he had become dangerous.

From the safety of an upstairs bedroom she studied the horses in the fields. They were old, maybe a 100 years in human terms, but behaved much younger. The stallion and the mare often galloped together. The vet had found nothing wrong with them; he marveled at their energy and health.

Observed more closely, though, the horses were covered with scars; they bit and kicked. Instantaneously, they seemed to revert to angry animals. One of them had kicked her.

The problem lay in their temperaments. Could equines turn moody? This pair appeared to be.

They charged into the plastic fence almost as though they wished to die, as if they resented the longevity the drug had given them.

Serious biotechnological issues had to be resolved.

How long should the nags be allowed to survive? Already they were a medical miracle but they might jeopardize the safety of her other horses.

Perhaps the same question applied to superannuated people. Should they be put away?

Somebody had to kill him. She?

Unless he had become immortal (with two "m's").

What did she know about immortality?

The gods, of course, were immortal by definition. They endured forever like the river and the sky, unless people lost faith in them. Then they vanished.

Science was their modern counterpart. The gods had been able to defy death with impunity. Could science make that claim?

The experiment had partially succeeded, both with animals and humans. He was the proof.

But she stood in the way. He'd have to settle for immortality with one "m".

If her bullet missed, she would be sacrificed, however, and he might go on, more or less endlessly, a triumph of modern science.

She'd had a chance of stopping him but failed.

PART I

▼

DISCOVERY

CHAPTER 1

▼

Professor Geoffrey Mulheran, an angelic fringe of white hair surrounding his bald dome, character lines on his pink face, wandered into Freddie's lab at Columbia Medical School. He resembled photos of Linus Pauling, twice a Nobel Laureate, that he had seen. An eminent molecular physicist who'd written textbooks and contributed countless articles to scientific journals, Geoff pushed 60. Freddie had been a graduate student of his and considered the prof her mentor.

"Fredericka," he said, always refusing to abbreviate her name, "I've received an electronic whatchamacallit."

"E-mail?" She grinned. The prof was always on top of the latest scientific discoveries but contemptuous of what he considered gadgetry.

"From a certain Noah Greenberg who identifies himself as a biochemist at Cold Spring Harbor Labs on Long Island." A pedant, Geoff was scrupulous with details.

"They perform gene studies there?"

"As part of the Human Genome Project," Mulheran said matter-of-factly.

Freddie was rinsing glasswork and putting the beakers and flasks on a cart for the maintenance crew to finish. She sat on a stool, brushed a blond hair from her smock and said, for nothing better, "They're coding millions of genes."

"And this Greenberg fellow has stumbled onto a gene with an unusual structure. He thinks it might have unique possibilities."

"Wouldn't the lab own the gene since it was discovered there?"

"Not necessarily. He was probably using his own time. Nights, weekends. Anyway, the gene will probably amount to nothing."

"But you're interested?"

"The gene produces a novel protein. Greenberg's unable to supply the exact chemical composition or the precise utility…"

"If there is one. Ninety-nine percent of the genetic material sequenced thus far has no apparent application and seems to be junk. Maybe it's there in case other genes are destroyed."

"Elementary, my dear." The Prof cocked his head. "Still, I wish we could understand the superfluous DNA. Nature's backup system is almost unbelievable. But the protein might conceivably have a use and this Greenberg chap has asked us to investigate."

"Why, should we?"

"Well, reputation, I suppose," Mulheran said modestly.

"You mean your reputation."

"I persevere, I admit."

The prof couldn't resist exploring theoretical trails even though they mostly led nowhere. She sometimes wished he was more practical but then she wouldn't be his lab detective. "Me, you mean," Freddie said sharply.

A smile wreathed Mulheran's face. "Are your decks clear?"

"What am I, a goddam sailor? I have to swab down from our previous experiment. Then I'm free, I guess."

In fact, she wanted a rest.

"How much time would be required, do you think?"

It would have taken anyone else a month but Freddie was the fastest lab gun in West Harlem. "Give me two fucking weeks."

Geoff's watery blue eyes regarded her solemnly. "No reason for profanity, my dear."

"I'll need rodents again and that's why I'm cursing. I hate the damn things."

Not for the first time, it occurred to Freddie she might have preferred being a man. Men used profanity all they liked and nobody objected.

And that wasn't all. Women tended to cry (a means of relieving tension, scientists claimed) but Freddie hated tears and refused to shed them. To her, tears were a sign of weakness, a quality she associated with females.

Well, not herself. Who did she identify with, males? Power instead of feminine helplessness. Why hadn't she been born a man?

*　　*　　*　　*

Packed in dry ice, the DNA fragments arrived by FedEx from Cold Spring Harbor. She opened the package, removed the vial, dumped the ice into a sink and let boiling water pour over it.

It took Freddie an endless week to produce enough of the protein to give the rats—cloning up Greenberg's gene using the polymerase chain reaction (invented by a California biochemist and surfer, Kery Mullis, who won the Nobel Prize for his efforts). She then inserted the gene into another nonpathogenic simian virus she'd grown in culture tubes. (Because it lacked reproductive machinery, the virus required a host, E.Coli bacteria, also nonpathogenic, to replicate itself.) The protein was then extracted from the genetic material.

Freddie threw the liquid into a homogenizer and beat the shit out of it for several hours. She then centrifuged the glop and separated the protein on an electronic gel. The result: a tiny dot at the end of a test tube filled with extraneous material.

She freeze-dried the protein dot which would be cloned and mixed with ordinary rat chow and fed to the study group.

Twenty years ago the technique would have seemed the wildest science fiction, but now the procedure was so routine Freddie could almost have followed it in her sleep.

These days practically anything organic could be cloned—that was, in the Greek, "branched", even, theoretically, humans.

The only rodents available from the Animal Storage Unit had been specially bred for experiments in senescence. Maybe the rodents could be kept alive for a couple of weeks but not without hardening of the arteries, tumors, vision impairment, osteoporosis, arthritis, loss of energy and other conditions associated with aging.

She stored the vial in the specimen refrigerator, where food was forbidden, with the familiar biosymbol and a handwritten warning: "DO **NOT** TOUCH. CONTENTS MAY BE BIOHAZARDOUS!"

Because, according to Mulheran, tests had shown the obscure simian virus was benign, causing at worst mild flu and headaches, Freddie had taken minimal precautions: a 5-micron particle filter over her nose and mouth, double latex gloves and a big, stainless steel vacuum hood to suck whatever had been in the FedEx box and spew it through a vent in the roof of the medical school. When the stuff reached the *bodegas* and auto parts stores of Dominican Harlem, it would be far too diluted to cause harm.

But the monkey virus made Freddie uneasy. She'd read somewhere that a virus could bind to a protein. Viruses tended to cause disease. And viruses spread, the very reason they existed.

The aging rats proved no problem. Technicians carried the cages from the storage unit in the basement. One group of ten rats would be the study group to be fed the protein; the other ten, the controls, would receive a placebo—a shot of saline solution in place of the protein.

She was preparing the injections when Greenberg called, inviting her to lunch.

Perhaps Freddie shouldn't accept. Her humor concealed raw nerves so why rock Noah's ark? But was this the time for corny jokes?

No. Genes were basic to life.

CHAPTER 2

▼

Freddie felt apprehensive as noon approached. That she knew few single men was because she concentrated so much on work and never had time for fun.

Or what others called fun. The truth was, she easily got bored. TV, the movies, Broadway shows, art galleries, usually failed to live up to expectations. Alcohol always left her cold. She suffered from what the French referred to as *cafard*—the blues.

Sex would have roused her from lassitude but she didn't have a boyfriend or even prospects. Most men bored her as well, Freddie had to admit. She had nothing against them personally; she just hadn't met one who excited her in ages. Or had she ever?

Perhaps she was anhedonistic, experienced pleasure rarely if at all.

Maybe she was too much of a perfectionist when it came to the opposite sex, too demanding. When she fell in love she'd fall hard, she thought—forfeit her good judgment, her objectivity. But she hadn't met a guy who lived up to her standards except Prof Mulheran and he was ancient. Would Noah also prove to be boring? She feared he would.

So, on shaking hands with him, Freddie wondered whom she'd anticipated—a scientist in shining armor? A tall, attractive male, single of course, a trailblazer, like Francis Crick or James Watson, co-founders of Cold Spring Harbor Labs and co-discoverers of the double helix molecule, the basis of our understanding of DNA. Yes, Freddie had rather hoped to meet a more flamboyant type.

Of medium height, Noah wore pedestrian clothes, jeans and a denim jacket—it was early summer—and wire-rimmed glasses. With a long nose, large ears and a downcast expression, he was far from handsome. She noticed he limped a bit as they walked to Pedro's Dominican (what else in Spanish Harlem?) Restaurant, near 168th and Broadway, where the hospital was.

Greenberg said he'd heard of Freddie from Mulheran who'd described her as being extremely capable.

"The Prof exaggerates."

"And you're too modest." He seemed almost in awe of her.

"Modest isn't how I'd describe myself," she said.

"What word would you use if you had to pick just one?"

"Bold, maybe. You?"

"Shy, I guess," he responded

"I suspect people always say the opposite about themselves from what is true. So, deep down, you're bold and I'm shy," she said.

"Possibly."

They'd reached the restaurant and, while Noah hesitated, Freddie grabbed a table. He struck her as rather bland until the conversation turned to science and then his face lit up. "Breakthroughs are constant in biochemistry. We're achieving so much that was never dreamed of."

"The same is true in my field," she said. "I specialize in mammalian proteins."

"How about *my* protein?"

Freddie rolled her eyes. "I'd just finished purifying the stuff when you called."

Noah laughed. "I'm being too pushy. I ask too many questions. For instance, do you exercise?"

"Sure. I jog, ride a stationery bike and lift weights. Want a feel? My bicep, of course."

He touched her arm. "Wow."

"And I climb stairs."

"Good. I....How old are you?"

"You shouldn't inquire, but I was 28 when last I bothered to count."

"You seem younger," he said.

"My face or how I act?"

"You could be a photographic model," Noah said wistfully, as if women such as Freddie were beyond his reach.

"I'm not like asshole models who pose semi-nude with rodents."

"You despise rats?"

"Only what happens to them. I want to cry when an experiment's finished and the rats must be sacrificed."

"Beheaded, that is," he said.

"I despise euphemisms."

"Like 'golden years', 'senior citizens', or 'aging process' instead of just 'growing old'," he said.

"Of course!"

Noah seemed to want to change the subject "Is Freddie your real name?"

She shook her head. "Fredericka. Fredericka Ferguson. My initials are FF, as in 'fast forward'. I took the cue and shortened my name to Freddie. Fredericka has too many syllables. So does my father's name, Frederick."

She nibbled at the eggs rancheros and spooned sugar into the iced tea; Noah took a forkful of rice and beans with chunks of pork. "Where's your father?"

"He lives in New Jersey. He's retired, a recluse on his little farm, almost a hermit. I'd help financially but I'm strapped."

"They don't pay much at Cold Spring Harbor either. It would be wonderful to have serious dough. How about your mother?"

"She's dead. From cancer. Grief, I think, caused Daddy to go off the deep end. He lost a small fortune gambling in Atlantic City and he'd always been cautious."

"Ferguson is Irish, right?"

"Uh-huh."

"That must account for your green eyes."

"Although Mom was of Nordic extraction," Freddie chatted. "She pushed me socially. I went to boarding school and had a coming-out party. I ate better food then. We had a French chef named Hortense who prepared soufflés and bili-bi."

"Huh?"

"Chilled mussel soup. She had a wart on her nose. Funny how you remember things from childhood. I couldn't have been more than five years old."

"Memory is strange, what it chooses to focus on."

"I wish I could recall everything. What about you?"

"I'm from the Lower East Side. My father was an Orthodox Jewish tailor."

"Where'd you go to school?"

"Erasmus High in Brooklyn where the family moved."

"I've never been to Brooklyn. To me it's like Siberia. And then?"

"NYU and Cornell on scholarships. I also worked as a waiter—a gimp waiter."

"Are you observant?"

"Of our laws? I attend a synagogue." He glanced down at his plate. "But then…"

"The pork?"

"…I eat pork. But I follow most of our customs. My mother would be shocked if she knew I was having lunch with a *shiksa*."

"What's a *shiksa*?"

"A Christian girl."

His gaze seemed to travel from her rounded forehead to her wideset eyes to the impudent nose to her mouth whose short upper lip conveyed both humor and an almost childlike determination.

"Much less married one, I suppose."

"Marriage is out of the question."

"Are you gay?"

"Of course not. I have a serious medical problem."

She recalled the limp. "Nothing communicable, I hope."

"No. Pompe's Disease runs in the family. That's one reason I'm so interested in genes. I have the adult type of Pompe's, less severe than the infantile or juvenile varieties, though still not fun. Basically, my muscles are slowly shrinking. I consulted the top guy in the field and all he could explain was, 'Noah, your muscles have started to atrophy. No one can predict how fast they'll go. The onset varies: you could be crippled by the time you're 40.' Big help, huh?"

Though slender and slightly stooped Greenberg appeared in good health. "Do you mind if I ask how old *you* are?"

"That's what most doctors want to know when they learn about the disease. I'm 36."

"Does age mean a lot to you?"

"Age doesn't count nearly as much as attitude. I guess you could call me a philosophic skeptic, like Protagoras."

"Who?"

"A pre-Plato Greek. Stoic and Sophist—a Sophist could argue any side of an argument…"

"Don't condescend. I know what they were."

"Protagoras' position was that we should not believe in what our senses tell us. You think the floor is firm, and then it suddenly caves in."

"From an earthquake?"

"The cause doesn't matter. Protagoras' point was we have to be skeptical of received wisdom."

"Okay."

"Protagoras was very important. Plato combined Protagoras with Heraclites and came up with the notion that all things are in the process of *becoming*, including knowledge. That opened the door to the theory of relativity and quantum mechanics. If things are constantly changing, nothing stays the same. Today's truth may be tomorrow's folly. We should learn to be skeptical about what we're told. There's always hope."

Yes. Always hope. Her father had told her that and she had mostly believed him, though sometimes her faith had been dashed on the reef of despair. The challenge for Freddie was to keep things in perspective, to realize life should be embraced as a totality, not squandered because of problems like aging.

But Noah had an incurable disease and she said, "Hope for Pompe's?"

"Maybe. I'm not a determinist, even when it comes to genes."

"You mean?"

"Human behavior isn't foreordained. We have some control over our destinies. We can become almost anything we want if we have the will."

"'Man is the measure of all things'? Except when women differ from men."

"There is no objective truth. That's why I believe in tradition."

They walked slowly back to the hospital and Freddie gave Noah a tour of the lab. He asked no questions about the protein or the procedures but only whether he could see her again—a *real* date. She nodded matter-of-factly and Noah, seeming pleased, returned to Cold Spring Harbor on the train.

She found him tedious but brave. Even noble in his doomed fight against Pompe's. What did she value most in a man? Truth was, she hadn't decided.

Men had found Freddie attractive for as long as she could recall. She'd never tried to take advantage of her femininity—she kept that on hold. She seemed forever preoccupied with more important matters. In graduate school, several young men had displayed more than a passing interest but though she earned a reputation for being friendly, she'd been unable to reciprocate.

Would the same happen with Noah? Uh-huh.

Were *she* a man, she'd have known how to handle women like her.

But what kind of man was Noah? Good, she judged. But suppose she was wrong?

And suppose her judgment of men was generally wrong? That might lead to disaster.

CHAPTER 3

▼

The control rats displayed Dewling's Syndrome—their eyes were murky, with fatty deposits in the corners—and they moved lethargically. They no longer bothered to groom themselves. The study group, also predestined to age fast, scampered in their cages, eyes bright, coats shiny, always sniffing. "They should be aging by now and they aren't, Freddie said to herself. To Carlos, the Latino she'd just hired, she said: "You've been feeding the study group the special diet?"

"Yes," he said.

Carlos had long flowing brunette curls, large brown eyes set in a tan complexion, delicate ears, small white hands as graceful as a woman's, a neat, pointed black chin beard, pearly teeth.

"The protein doesn't seem to have hurt them. Let's sacrifice a few from both groups and post 'em."

"Post?"

"Dissect. Conduct a post-mortem. *Comprende?*"

Carlos, a grad student, understood all too well. "I can't bear the sight of blood," he whimpered.

"You'll have to learn."

Carlos put his fingers in the pockets of his lab coat defiantly.

Freddie sighed. "Okay, I'll do it."

She held her nose and, with a double-gloved hand, dipped into the study-group's cage for a frisky rat. She grabbed a squirming body and, with a syringe, administered an intraperitoneal injection of phenobarbital. The rodent went limp. Then she shoved it against the spring-loaded knife, decapitating it. The other rats became agitated—they could smell the blood.

"Little Carloses," Freddie muttered. She left the body in the stainless steel sink to drain.

She had less luck with the second rat; she lost her grip and instead of executing the miserable creature, she cut off its snout. The rodent—she evidently hadn't injected enough phenobarb—unexpectedly strong, ran around the lab bench, bleeding profusely, then jumped to the floor and attempted to hide behind the 800-pound centrifuge which had required four men from engineering to install. Small wonder she hated lab rats.

Her arm was muscular but thin and she managed to retrieve the animal which had died. Thank God!

She wielded a scalpel on the bodies as she dictated to Carlos who jotted notes: "Bone tissue...respiratory system...liver...heart, perfect...color normal. Unremarkable, except...No indication these individuals are past their prime. I repeated the posts on control rodents. These individuals don't look so good. Tissue much less firm, bones grayer; joint movement weaker, tendons less elastic."

The autopsies had required all of five minutes. Perched on a stool, tensely rubbing her cheek, she phoned the prof.

*   *   *   *

Up on the tenth floor, Geoffrey Mulheran had arrived at his office with a queasy sensation in his stomach, blurred vision and other symptoms he identified as a hangover. Didn't the medical docs call it alcohol withdrawal syndrome? A closet drinker, he'd consumed far too much vodka the previous night in his lonely apartment. He lacked the ability to stop but AA was for weaklings, not him. Even brilliant scientists have foibles, he consoled himself.

Nausea had forced him to skip breakfast, but after a skimpy lunch washed down with black coffee, his head was clear. When Fredericka called, he took the lift down to the eighth floor. She'd sounded alarmed. Perhaps Greenberg's protein had poisoned the rodents and the experiment had been for naught.

What did he expect? His existence in recent years seemed a breeding ground for pessimism. The divorce, the drinking...which was the causal factor? Had he become an alcoholic because his wife had left him or the other way round? Hard to tell. And then the problem with the anti-cholesterol molecule. Because of recklessness engendered by the divorce or heavy drinking....aaiiii...if another opportunity arrived Mulheran resolved not to make mistakes. He'd be alert to every chance in a world filled with untrustworthy bastards.

For how long had he experienced the universe as bleak if not hostile? Since childhood, he supposed, or earlier, in the womb, programmed by his genes. What accounted for, assuming such existed, genetic memory? He hadn't had an earlier life, he was certain, but his primitive ancestors might have been hunters who fought wild animals. Today's wild animals were in business and that was why they upset him. When that genetic strain ran out, true Socialism would emerge.

Yes. Cooperation instead of hostility. Unselfishness instead of greed.

Geoff would never engage in deception. He was too advanced.

$$* \qquad * \qquad * \qquad *$$

The arrow pointed to the eighth floor, and preoccupied, Mulheran almost forgot to get off. He went to Fredericka's lab and she brought him up to speed, pointing at the two groups of rats. He knew the setup. The study-group was energetic, the controls fat and listless. Four dissected rodents lay on the bench—the lab worker hadn't yet disposed of them. "What's so urgent?" he asked.

She shrugged, her inclination toward excitement tempered by scientific caution. "I don't pretend to understand but the rats that eat the special protein are in far better shape than the controls. I posted members of both groups and their organs prove the point. The study rats have completely ceased aging, like in Shangri-la."

"Pardon?"

"Shangri-la. The hidden place in the Himalayas, Bhutan, I think, where people never grow old."

"Never?"

"Unless they leave the Tibetan monastery. Then they instantly age."

"Sounds far-fetched," Mulheran said crossly.

"It's fiction after all. And we're talking here of rats, not people," Freddie said.

Geoff examined the cages again. "The only difference is Greenberg's protein? How old would you estimate the study rodents are in human terms?"

"It's hard to make a meaningful comparison but they're late middle-aged in my opinion."

"Like the baby boomer generation, so-called?"

"On the verge of retirement, except rodents don't play golf or watch TV."

"Not yet at least. I've heard there are commercials for cats, so why not rodents? They're as smart." Mulheran chuckled and plopped onto a stool. "Do you want to continue testing?"

"By all means."

The molecular physicist scratched his bald dome and seemed to ponder. "Who knows? Maybe we've found a Fountain of Youth? What if Greenberg's protein halts human aging as well?"

Freddie glanced at Carlos. "Shouldn't we refer to the substance as Protein X?"

"Yes. Secrecy must be preserved."

*   *   *   *

Mulheran knew he should climb the steps for exercise but he was in a hurry now and took the lift. He had to make a call.

He had a compelling reason for secrecy. After almost a decade, much of it working on a screen that flipped thousands of chemical compounds, he'd stumbled on one that might reduce High Density Lipids (HDLs) in cholesterol. All drugs were molecules but not all molecules were drugs, and the drug molecule had to be sufficiently unique to patent and capable of reaching the target, another molecule. Hundreds of lab hours followed. He had understood the new drug's potential and proudly presented his findings at a medical conference as a cure for hyperlipidemia. He'd even cited the formula.

When he'd descended from the lectern a well-groomed man had asked to see his notes. He must have had a minicamera because, a few weeks later, Mulheran learned—oh God!—the formula had been patented by a pharmaceutical company which claimed to have been working on the product all along.

Mulheran had been seeking investors for the new drug and he'd had a glimpse of financial independence. He longed to quit teaching and devote himself to science.

A drug that put a stop to aging would be an outstanding product, the kind that placed biotech outfits on the map and made stockholders instant millionaires.

Leaving the elevator, Geoff pictured the advertisements:

A LONGER LIFE IS TO DIE FOR

No, a bit grim that.

ENJOY A LONGER LIFE THROUGH…

Of course, to enjoy longer life one would have to be in near-perfect health, as the aging study rats seemed to be.

Mulheran knew his excitement over Protein X was premature and should be contained. Still, discovery thrilled him: major science proceeded not so much through luck or inspiration but by following clues. And the clues left by the rodents led him to the view that aging could be forestalled almost indefinitely.

Fredericka would insist on more extensive proof but Protein X must somehow affect the gene or genes responsible for growing old and ultimately, death. Yes, the death gene. That would be a landmark finding.

Mulheran wanted to be part of the action but he lacked sizeable assets and a credit rating so the banks wouldn't lend him the enormous amount of money such an enterprise would need and, for obvious reasons, he distrusted the pharmaceutical companies.

He remembered his motto, cited below his listing in *Who's Who In American Science*: "Genius counts but perseverance pays off." If only he'd persevered in his marriage instead of giving up. Heartbreak might have been avoided, the pain proved unnecessary. Here he was, a middle or late-middle—Christ, how our society plastered you with labels so advertisers could decide how to pigeonhole their dough—aged scientist and alone.

Maybe, if he could regain personal self-confidence, he'd try to find another wife. A great deal depended on the protein. All right, he'd persevere.

Ransacking his files, Mulheran at last stumbled on the name he'd been trying to remember, a man who'd been deeply interested in the cholesterol product and pledged to raise the necessary capital. Zygmunt Szaba's background was somewhat obscure. Zig, as he called himself, had been born in Poland. He had migrated to the States many years before. He was an excellent amateur scientist with a keen grasp of theory. Just the sort of fellow Mulheran was now hellbent on locating.

Zig specialized in rounding up European risk capital. God knew who his backers were.

Could Szaba be trusted? Normally, Geoff wouldn't have crawled into bed with such a chap but...

He must listen to the 'but'.

But?

But now that he spotted gold under the microscope he decided to take a chance with the secret. He was desperate, he realized. This might be his last chance and he mustn't fail.

Mulheran remembered Zig as tall, trim, nice-looking, with a habit of mussing his wavy gray hair. He was snappily dressed, confident of his own abilities and, well, somewhat slick and self-centered. Ego went with his territory.

He had to be in his mid-fifties by then but probably still looked younger. Mulheran felt ancient by comparison. Yes, he'd aged prematurely. He looked exactly as his father had—bald, thick glasses, deep facial lines.

But Mulheran was more vigorous than his dad had been.

Zig was vigorous too, the kind of fellow you could count on for immediate results, Geoff thought.

Nonetheless, having made a fool of himself with the anti-cholesterol product's chemical formula, Geoff was hesitant. He wouldn't reveal his conclusion, wouldn't discuss the results with Szaba in any detail but let the experiment speak for itself. If Mulheran were any judge of character, Szaba would flip. He'd recognize a great business opportunity when he saw one.

If not? Mulheran wondered at what stage perseverance ran out.

*   *   *   *

A few miles away, as a mathematical crow would count, Zygmunt Szaba was traversing Central Park in his chauffeur-driven limo. The destination, a dentist, his third appointment in a month. His teeth were laden with cavities, as his mother's had been. She'd had deplorable teeth too. The dentist blamed Szaba for poor oral hygiene—failure to floss, use a water jet, etc. But Zig knew better. One's teeth reflected heredity. A weak excuse, his dentist told him.

Sooner or later, arguably later, Zig would need implants, which meant bone mass would have to be inserted, his sinuses raised. A messy, painful procedure. He would almost have preferred to be an animal that grew replacement teeth, like sharks, he thought. Yes, maybe he had a few shark genes.

An idle thought popped into his mind: perhaps suicide would be preferable to oral surgery. Suicide, why not? The notion had occurred to him before. The act might be acceptable if it were attached to a noble cause.

*   *   *   *

The answering service directed his calls to the cell phone in the Daimler. Zig had deals pending, *if* they came to anything, and he couldn't afford to be out of touch, but the caller's identity astonished him, a man whom Szaba hadn't heard from in years. A famous scientist, Geoffrey Mulheran, had discovered a drug that appeared to lower HDL in the bloodstream, Zig recalled, potentially a terrific money-maker. The idiot had revealed the formula and somebody else obtained the patent. Szaba, who'd invested time and effort to persuade his backers to finance the deal, had sworn never to engage in business with the naïve professor again.

Still, after Geoff's greeting, "Hello, Mr. Szaba" Zig heard the words "Enjoy longer life through…." and shifted the phone to his better ear.

"A possible product?"

"You be the judge of that," Mulheran said.

"Give me a better clue," Szaba said.

"A protein substance."

"So?"

"A protein that might affect human aging. That's all I intend to tell you. An experiment here at the hospital conducted by—"

For the nth time Zig canceled the appointment—the dentist would be livid—and instructed his driver to take him to Columbia Hospital. Rush-hour traffic crawled on Broadway and Szaba sat in the rear seat, head lowered, eyes shut.

A man of his talents and insights ought not to be in the soup. He was strong, resourceful, clever, industrious and so forth. He should have foreseen the savage decline in the value of biotech stocks just after he'd borrowed a bundle of money to buy more. His frugal Polish ancestors would have been ashamed of him but there he was, in debt. How quickly biotech stocks had declined in value!

Summer rentals paid for the Massachusetts castle but that left the luxurious apartment in the Carlyle, the condo in Paris. He needed them to impress his visitors, the greedy ones with huge sums to invest.

His only real function was to scout out opportunities in the biotech field. He read countless medical journals, talked endlessly on the phone to experts, pacing back and forth until he'd worn a trail in the Persian carpet. He wasn't perfect—perfection, elusive as ever, remained his goal—but he was good enough not to be in his present financial plight.

Simply to leave his bed in the morning cost him, on an annualized basis, a half million a year and his savings were being rapidly depleted.

He hadn't had a new investment idea in what seemed forever. Perhaps biotechnology had run out of attractive notions. They were promising a cure for almost *anything*. How could that be? What about the common cold?

"…affect human aging," Mulheran had claimed. Surely not for the worse. Everyone expected to live longer in the Third Millennium—a cliché by now—and if that was all Mulheran promised Zig might as well go home.

Still, perhaps the protein substance would prove miraculous, like penicillin or the polio vaccine. Zig had to know.

But he was ahead of himself. He'd have to observe the experiment and meet this Ferguson dame who worked at the lab bench. Mulheran had told him of the schools she'd attended. Mulheran had promised not to be intrusive. Szaba would have to draw his own conclusions.

The Daimler drew up at an imposing marble-and-glass facade. They'd reached the hospital.

＊　　＊　　＊　　＊

Ferguson's lab was on the eighth floor. As Zig anticipated, few or no provisions had been taken for security. The door wasn't locked and he walked in unannounced.

He wasn't certain what sort of woman he'd expected to encounter—probably a middle-aged lab technician—but the female standing at the bench met his strict standards of perfection. She was not only young but almost unbearably beautiful with straight Greco-Roman features and lively green eyes. Wisps of golden hair peeked from beneath a green surgical cap and made her seem girlish. Her skin was unblemished. Thin cheeks descended to a mouth with a short upper lip, suggesting sensuousness, and a rather pointed chin, indicating a stubborn streak, perhaps. Physiognomy was to Szaba an excellent index of character. In any case, she was an American dish.

She removed her lab coat, on the verge of going home, Zig thought, as he stole a look at her body, tall and thin with narrow curved hips and small pointed breasts. She was precisely the sort of woman he craved. A line from the Polish poet, Jan Szflaudynger, crossed his mind:

> No magnet is as effective
> As the magnet of a beautiful body
> Requests will not give you permission
> Because women like a conqueror

To display lust, however, struck him as crude and tactless. Instead he'd hide his interest and come on cool. Patience eventually paid off. Zig had vast experience with women.

> When I am next to a beautiful woman
> I keep my breath deep.

"I'm Zygmunt Szaba, Dr. Ferguson."

"Why are you here?" she cried, examining the pin-striped business suit, hand-painted tie and gold cufflinks.

"Professor Mulheran sent me to inspect the lab."

"Are you an efficiency expert or something?"

"No. I'm a businessman. Think of me as a philanthropist if you wish."

"Oh."

"And I have a sincere interest in science. Geoff Mulheran told me your results are provocative."

Her nostrils flared. "Well, I believe you find *me* provocative," she said in a surly tone.

Szaba, trying to soothe her, turned to the rodents in their cages. "Are they in good shape?"

"Half are. They're young-old rats."

"And the other half?"

"They're tired." she said warily.

Scientists were generally disinclined to share information on their current projects, Szaba knew. She reminded him of Botticelli's Venus on a clamshell. The painter had attempted to convey, in Szaba's opinion, the dual nature of women. They could make love to you or close up tight.

He wanted to bed this woman then and there, but only said, "Have any died?"

"Only the ones we sacrificed."

"For the research?"

"Mmmm." He enjoyed the way her lips curved.

"And what did you learn?" he quizzed.

"Well…." Freddie faltered. "What kind of philanthropist are you?"

Szaba smiled. "Benefactors are all the same. They give money away."

Freddie gestured toward the rodents. "All the rats are programmed to age but these *seem* to be doing much better than those."

"Which is which?"

"Shit, can't you tell?" She jabbed a finger and laughed proudly, picking up a study-group rodent and nuzzling it.

"Have the rats received different treatment?" he said politely.

A smile limned her lean face. "The frisky rats have been fed a special protein and I cuddle them."

"May I inquire what the protein is?"

Freddie rebuffed him. "Ask the prof."

"I shall." He bowed at the waist, a courtly mannerism she had never seen outside of Cary Grant movies. "Thank you for your time, Dr. Ferguson. You've obviously been creative here."

$$* \qquad * \qquad * \qquad *$$

In the silver Daimler once more Szaba made a rapid series of calls. The first was to Mulheran who waited anxiously.

"Tell me what the study rats are fed," he barked.

Mulheran's reply was inaudible. Was it the cell phone? "Again?" Szaba commanded.

"I mentioned a protein."

"Can it be duplicated?"

"Yes."

"And the stuff truly confers longevity in rats."

"It's still very early in our work on the protein, but so far the study rates haven't aged."

"Would it be effective with humans?"

"I don't know. We'd have to conduct a lot more research. Which would be expensive."

"Are there precedents?"

"Of course. Scientists have recently succeeded in postponing age in threadworms and fruit flies through genetic manipulation," Mulheran said.

"The telomerse gene."

"Correct. The enzyme it releases enables cells to grow and divide indefinitely. The problem is how to insert telomerse genes into the body so tissues will accept them."

"We'd remain youthful then?"

"But such technology is years off. Our discovery is in real time."

"Wouldn't the hospital pay for the new research?"

"They'd insist on owning the patent rights."

"Uh-huh. We'd find a way around the problem. How about your assistant? Tell me about her…will she stay on the job?"

"Fredericka is committed to the project and she's utterly reliable."

"Inform her I'm behind the project."

"Wonderful!"

Zig offered to fund the protein project for up to fifty thousand dollars but he had conditions. Mulheran agreed to them.

Zig's next call was to Poland where it was after 2 a.m.

"Daiendobry kto mowi...?" (Who's calling?")

"Zig."

"Oho, jaka cena?" (How much?)

The risk was high, potential profits immense. Warsaw guaranteed $150,000 seed money.

Zig next phoned his private security man. A woman named Ferguson worked in the lab. Szaba had to know if she could be trusted. Had she some kind of criminal record? Ever cheated on exams? Would she steal? Had she a weakness others might exploit? Was she a substance abuser?

His last call was to a florist who delivered round the clock.

Early next morning Freddie found orchids at the reception desk with a card signed "S". "To a remarkable woman," the card read. Yesterday's handsome visitor—he *was* handsome, goddammit—must have sent the flowers.

*   *   *   *

That day, at the prof's insistence, a double lock was installed on the lab door to which only Mulheran, Freddie, Carlos and the maintenance people had keys.

Mulheran had asked Freddie to identify the protein's molecular structure, a first step toward obtaining a patent for a biological product. She thought this premature—they weren't ready to prove the protein retarded aging, but he was the boss and he seemed eager.

The gene, already mapped by Greenberg, dictated a specific sequence of amino acids, the building blocks of proteins. But the protein wasn't just a chain but a complex structure with unique folds and twists. Just as a completed building looks far different than in an architect's blueprints, so with the protein.

One technique to tease out this structure involved feeding the sequence into a computer, using information like basic polarities and other aspects of the amino acids to create a 3-D picture. With more than 100 gigabytes of memory, the computer generated a mathematically-calculated estimate of the protein's appearance—a shining globule; a multicolored microscopic planet of ridges, curves and valleys. Wow, Freddie thought, staring at the printout.

She showed the graph to the prof who said, "Remarkable. So many secrets crammed into a speck of matter. Just think, we're composed of those."

"Can we ever know ourselves?"

"Not really if we're nothing more than a collection of amino acids."

"What about evil?"

Mulheran shrugged his narrow shoulders. "I don't pretend to understand."

"Maybe we have to have faith."

"In nature?"

"Or God."

"Strange," he said. "The more we penetrate our tiny universe the more necessary the God idea seems to account for nature. Even for me and I'm an atheist."

"God in the sense of a grand designer?"

"Something like that, yes."

"And when the design falls apart?"

"Blame a flaw like myself." Mulheran referred to his drinking, she thought.

Freddie sighed. To her a flawed design would be represented by a murderer, a cold-blooded killer. Of course, she'd hadn't encountered one and never would in her line of work.

Although she knew how to use a gun, Freddie would have hated being a cop. The only blood she ever expected to see would be drawn from lab animals for clinical tests.

*   *   *   *

In assaying the protein, she relied also on an old-fashioned technique, growing the protein in crystals, chemically fracturing the crystals like ice cubes and scanning them through an electron microscope. Examining the weird images was no less exciting than watching the first photos from the Sojourner Mars mission.

Yes, man's best hope lay in science. Where else could we learn the truth? But she thought of Noah's skepticism.

Carlos took copious notes. She refused to let him use a tape recorder. The tapes could too easily be duplicated. Why should that concern her? she asked herself. Because Carlos might have a design flaw, might be tempted to dispose of the purloined tapes for cash. (She couldn't bring herself to use the word "stolen".)

The gorgeous Latino had to be aware they were testing a compound both for the patent and the U.S. Food and Drug Administration approval, necessary if Mulheran was right and the protein really became a biological product. What would they name it? Freddie wondered.

It was bad enough that she distrusted Carlos and for no special reason except for underlying prejudice—he was guilty of Hispanic birth, was all. So maybe *she* had the design flaw.

And then she had Martha to contend with. Martha had been on welfare until the city ordered her to find work or lose her benefits. Freddie had conversed with the older woman in the hospital cafeteria where Martha washed cooking utensils.

She disliked the job—the lifting bothered her arthritic shoulder—and Freddie, having decided Martha was reliable, suggested she try the lab.

"What happens up there?"

"We experiment with rats."

Martha's wrinkled face sagged. She stroked her double chin with blunt fingernails. "No, no, no, I couldn't. I simply couldn't. I can't stand the sight of those nasty creatures."

"Actually, they're rather sweet, not like street rats, you know," Freddie said.

"Don't they bite?"

"Rarely."

Martha took the job. She always wore long sleeves which Freddie assumed was to protect her arms from the rodents. Prejudices died hard. Either that or she was hiding varicose veins.

On weekends, which Carlos had off, Martha fed the rats. (Freddie was usually there but Martha lightened her load.) Martha also performed unpleasant tasks—weighing the feces to check against food intake, measuring the water the rats drank, a safeguard against dehydration. Martha would pull their skins to observe elasticity.

Martha proved intelligent and submissive. She scrubbed the cage floors and kept the food and water containers filled while Carlos, who sometimes seemed more concerned with his coiffure, occasionally forgot.

Freddie never failed to marvel at the vagaries of human character, hers too, maybe. The rodents were always the same but people demonstrated eccentricities.

Was that genetic? Such an analysis seemed far out but no more far out than causing the test rodents to live well beyond their normal years. Science eventually would have to come to terms with normality: how should it be defined?—but in the meantime, she had to deal with quirky behavior.

Freddie first picked up a symptom when Martha came to the lab in a mink jacket. She claimed it had belonged to her aunt but Martha lived in a cheap apartment. Besides the mink was new and fashionable. Did Martha engage in shoplifting?

And might she steal loose change?

Having noticed coins seemed to be missing, Freddie carefully left five quarters on the lab bench when she and Carlos departed for lunch. When she returned, three of the quarters were gone.

To have validity, a controlled experiment had to be repeated. The next day, she left three quarters and one was swiped by Martha.

Freddie diagnosed kleptomania. Theft was a compulsion the overweight woman couldn't resist.

Perhaps, as Martha aged, the neurosis would disappear. But if Freddie confronted her, she'd lie and angrily deny the accusation and Freddie would have no choice but to discharge her. From then on, Freddie kept her change in her lab coat and said nothing.

She was secretive by nature and always had been, she knew. When had that characteristic appeared? Why did she have it?

Talk about neurosis!

She must have been neurotic as a child. She remembered hiding in the basement, staying there for hours on end, even as her parents cajoled her to emerge. She had a hiding place underneath the stairs and, though starving, she had refused to come out.

She'd hidden repeatedly and the psychologist her parents summoned figured Freddie needed more attention than the usual child.

Was that still the case?

If so, and if he pursued her with sex in mind, Szaba might understand and take advantage of her.

She'd only met him once but first impressions seldom went awry. He was sharp and might have penetrated the weakness behind her femininity. That made her want to sob, as females will. She hated being a woman, but not for long.

CHAPTER 4

▼

Posing as a headhunter, Len Veere, Szaba's private security man, went to Short Hills to investigate Fredericka. He was careful not to have anyone alert her father who owned a small farm nearby but was seldom there.

Veere pieced together her story from interviews and an article in the local paper. He noted the absence of close friends. She seemed to have been the solitary sort who preferred her own company.

She'd written poetry but burned it, she'd told a classmate who said to Veere, "Because the rhymes weren't good enough....She was a stickler for perfection." (Reading this later, Szaba wondered if he might have found a soulmate.)

She was a crack shot who practiced in the basement of her high school which had pistol classes. About that time she got a microscope and her interest turned to biology.

Ms. Ferguson had gone to boarding school but switched to a regular high school when her dad could no longer foot the bills. She seemed to have adjusted easily. She'd been valedictorian, graduating at the top of her class, and attended Sarah Lawrence where she graduated *magna cum laude* at the tender age of 21. MIT had awarded her a PhD in molecular biology and she did her post-doc work under Professor Mulheran.

"Didn't she have any weaknesses?" Veere asked the amiable principal who'd been there when Fredericks was a student.

The principal well remembered the girl. "She was famous for her looks and brilliance and I kept track of her. She was both a student activist and a cheer-leader until she suddenly dropped from sight."

"Why?"

"I shouldn't be telling you this, but she had a rare skin condition. It must have disappeared by now."

"What skin condition?"

"Ichthyosis."

"Say again."

"Ichthyosis."

"Would you write that down?"

The principal did so. He said, "She was born with it, but had a mild case."

Szaba had a medical dictionary and Veere had studied the pages. "A congenital disorder characterized by dryness and fishlike scaling of the skin," he scribbled.

Szaba skimmed Len's report and pronounced himself dissatisfied. Freddie seemed perfect, too perfect. "Hasn't she *any* problems?"

"You haven't finished what I gave you—the icky stuff."

"What is it?"

"A rash."

"Where?"

"Varies, the fella told me. Sometimes a faint patch on her waist, sometimes thick blotches on her cheek....It's totally based on nerves, he believes. If she's worried about how she'll look in a skimpy cheerleader's outfit the rash shows up on her belly but if she's gonna give a lecture it appears on her cheek."

Zig remarked, "Maybe she faked the rash to get out of cheerleading."

"She gave lectures at MIT though."

"Perhaps they were easy for her. I want her kept under surveillance. I can't take chances. The protein could become a billion dollar product. I have to trust the woman 100 percent."

"What makes you so sure you can't trust this Fredericka dame?"

"She's too suspicious."

"Is that bad?"

"Could be. I want my people to follow my orders without any questions, as my chauffeur does."

"But he's an idiot. You make me sound like some sort of slave, boss."

"You are, Len. Don't forget I could send you back to prison."

*   *   *   *

Mulheran had been attending a biotech conference and Freddie brought him up to date. "The protein doesn't affect young rats at all. It only seems to interfere with the older rodents' aging."

"How does that play out in human terms?"

"If you ask me, human aging, contrary to popular wisdom, commences at 30. Most people think you plateau at about 50, stay at the peak of your powers for a long while, then begin the slow slide into infirmity, but it just ain't the case. All the measures of strength reach their height at 30 then start dropping. Respiratory function, cardiac output, the works. Ever notice you never hear about a 50-year-old champion sprinter?"

"Yes, I've observed that."

"Athletes seldom retain their prowess beyond age 40."

"How about George Foreman?" Mulheran asked.

"You watch boxing, prof? But even he had to quit the ring."

"What are you getting at?"

"That the new drug won't do anything until the body is ready to accept it, which probably means the correct age to start taking Protein X is at 50 or later. Before that the stuff would be wasted."

"No need to give me a term paper, Fredericks. Have you observed side effects among the rodents?"

"None so far, but one has to keep in mind some of them might not appear for a considerable period. They don't show short-term effects, like bone-marrow suppression, such as you get from chemotherapy. But remember what happened with thalidomide. When doctors prescribed it for nausea in early pregnancy and they delivered infants with flippers for arms and legs. The study rats could remain energetic for years, then might drop dead from causes unknown."

"And then there's the prescription drug Seldane. The side effects didn't show up until at least 10,000 people had used the stuff," Mulheran said, rather anxiously.

"The FDA issued warnings and the manufacturer removed it from the market because a safer product was available," she reminded him.

"And you have pharmaceutical products, such as natural aspirin from willow tree bark and drugs made from tropical plants but all have side effects," Mulheran commented. "The new genomic drugs seek to avoid them. Well, thus far Protein X seems to lack toxicity, correct?"

"With zero side effects," Freddie repeated for emphasis' sake. "I'd like to start experimenting with higher animals—such as rhesus monkeys."

"If the results hold up, there's no reason the protein can't be mass produced," Mulheran said. He caressed his scalp; his eyes twinkled in anticipation of the big money he was bound to make; he rubbed his leathery hands.

"There's many a slip 'twist cup and lip'."

"Quite right. 'Never count your chickens before they hatch.' And so forth. But, Fredericka, we're onto something here."

"Yes," she said, suddenly frowning.

"What's the trouble?"

"I was thinking of Noah. It's *his* protein, after all."

"The pride of ownership, eh? Well, if any entity *owns* the protein, it's Mother Nature and she has surrendered the patent rights. They're up for grabs."

"That doesn't seem fair."

"Fairness is in the eyes of the beholder," Mulheran said.

"Know what? You're sometimes a real bastard, prof. Excuse me, please. No offense intended."

"And none taken. But you mustn't tell this Greenberg of what's happened with the protein. He's not in the, ahhh, loop."

Freddie swallowed her guilt. "Okay," she said, not really meaning it.

✳   ✳   ✳   ✳

Freddie realized she might be considered a co-conspirator. The judge was herself.

Where were the ethics her father had pounded into her? Could she navigate life without a moral compass? Was charm enough? No, not really but it helped.

She decided to inform Noah he was about to be swindled. That was how a he-man would have disposed of the matter. Maybe Freddie was a she-man.

✳   ✳   ✳   ✳

Szaba hadn't phoned—why? she wondered. Maybe despite the obvious flirtation with her, he wasn't that attracted. Or maybe he had a steady girl, even a wife. She'd never been involved with a married man and she didn't intend to start.

But Greenberg called just as Freddie was setting up the canine and monkey tests and she invited him to dinner to tell him of the potential rip-off. Perhaps Noah would display emotions. The only topic that had excited him so far, except maybe herself (which she remained skeptical of) was Protagoras, not much to base a relationship on. Was she seeking a love affair? Yes and no. Yes in the sense she was hungry for sex but that urge, so far, had centered on Szaba, she had to admit. Perhaps Noah would cause her to switch her affections.

No. A relationship might, undoubtedly would, be a distraction from her work which had always ranked first. Why couldn't she had both?

The few men Freddie had allowed into her life so far had proved demanding, usurped her time, intruded into her private space. Might Noah be different?

He wasn't her *beau idéal* in terms of looks or finesse but his courage intrigued her and she longed to understand where or how he'd found it.

Perhaps he concealed vital aspects of his personality as she did hers.

Freddie decided to give Noah a fighting chance. Maybe she'd be lucky for a change. Just thinking about his visit aroused her. She hoped she wasn't doomed to disappointment.

*   *   *   *

Her West Side apartment, within walking distance of the hospital, overlooked the Hudson River. The view was spectacular but you had to climb four flights of steps to see it.

The buzzer sounded and she heard Noah's tenor voice on the intercom. She pressed the button and admitted him. He arrived on the top floor and threw himself on the couch.

"Sorry," he gasped, audibly winded.

"What's the matter? Out of shape? I climb the steps couple of times a day."

"You don't have Pompe's Disease. I do my best but…"

"You require exercise, that's all. You claimed it was the type that might not progress."

"*Might,*" he said gloomily.

"Where's Protagoras when you need him? A Stoic conceals his suffering. Not you, though."

"I'm not in a philosophical mood today."

"You've lost courage?"

"Temporarily. The steps were like a mountain."

"But you made it to the top!"

"Without an oxygen tank," Noah said wryly.

Freddie was forced to decide whether to pity Noah or disregard his suffering. Because she enjoyed the man's sardonic humor and admired his scientific skills, she chose the latter course: to perceive a man—sick wasn't the right way to start a relationship.

She removed her flat-heeled shoes, lit candles and incense. "Want some pot?"

"Marijuana?"

The weed almost grows on the streets in Dominican neighborhoods."

"I'll pass."

She puffed on a hand-rolled joint. "Relax, Noah. Have fun for once."

Did *she*? Months, no years, had elapsed since she'd slept with boys, a couple of brief encounters. She hadn't even had orgasms because of resentment, she supposed. The guys were faceless now; she couldn't remember their names. She *had* considered Noah for a partner and she'd worn tight jeans and an off-the-shoulder blouse to show him her slender frame but something fell between them. Pompe's Disease—she could live with that. No. It was her knowledge of the miracle protein.

The study group rats remained alert when they should have long since succumbed to old age. Jesus Christ would have reached 66 had he avoided crucifixion and been fed the protein. The rodents had survived much longer than they should have. Was there a downside to that and Noah?

Here was a drug that could *really* transform the world: if humans lived 150 years the change would be astonishing. You'd maybe have philosopher kings and certainly trillionaires instead of mere billionaires; people would live to see multiple generations of descendants. Everyone who used the protein would be in perfect health

And all because of some frisky rodents.

She sucked in her breath, tempted to tell him of the experiment, the barrier would be removed.

But Freddie said nothing and she asked herself why.

At the last moment, her innate caution prevailed: Freddie decided she didn't know Greenberg well enough to trust him. If he threatened to sue, that might bring the experiment to a halt, a result she hadn't foreseen.

She said glumly, "I'm tempted to weep."

"What stops you?"

"Do you take me for a sissy? I dislike tears." Freddie frowned.

"Why?"

"Too feminine."

"So?"

"Hard to explain."

"Are you upset because of me?" Noah also frowned.

Men's egos were pathetic. Or was the proper word bathetic? Humorless, self-indulgent. They believed everything revolved around them. Noah *was* proving a source of annoyance.

"No. The lab work is at a critical stage."

"Is my protein viable?"

Freddie examined his face with mild disdain. "The question proves you're not a protein enzymologist. Viable? You mean labile? Stable at room temperature? Doesn't degrade over time? Doesn't immediately metabolize after it enters the body? Has a legitimate purpose there?"

Caught up in the terminology, Noah neglected to ask what the purpose of the experiment was.

Freddie paced the large, one-room apartment, a penthouse, literally house top. Far to the south, she could see the lights of New Jersey, her former home.

Cheap, computerized printouts of modern art masterpieces decorated the apartment's walls along with a photo of a lovely naked woman. The hardwood floor was strewn with rugs. The couch stood in the corner. An exercise bike flanked by weights occupied the opposite corner. Behind the counter food warmed in the oven. A wooden ladder led to a platform where Freddie slept. The gentle September rain pattered on the skylights.

Noah had started to speak but afraid he might resume the discussion about the protein, she interrupted him. "Are you hungry?"

"What's for dinner?" He sounded like a TV commercial.

"Salad, sweet potatoes and ham."

A scowl creased Noah's features. "I don't eat ham."

"Because you're Jewish? I thought...."

"I don't enjoy the taste of ham."

"But you have to eat!"

Noah shrugged.

"I'll fix spaghetti and there's wine."

"All right."

It occurred to her he might have brought a bottle. Or flowers. A trinket to demonstrate affection. Suddenly she felt imposed upon. Men were brutes.

And perhaps Noah had a secretive side, an aspect of his persona he wanted to conceal. A criminal record? Nonsense. But there was something about him she didn't like although she didn't know why.

Noah glanced at the platform. "I'll never find a taxi in this rain. I'll have to walk to the subway to get to Grand Central Station for my train to Cold Spring. Would you mind if I slept here?"

"Would I mind?" She screamed softly. "I'd sure as hell mind. Eat your supper and leave, Noah."

She was staring at New Jersey through the casement window wishing she still lived there, when Szaba called, inviting her to dinner on Saturday night. Remembering the orchids, and Noah's selfishness, she accepted at once.

Still, she wouldn't write Noah off completely. Despite his rough edges, he was *sympathique*. Could the same be said of Szaba?

Somehow he frightened her a little. She felt an impulse to hide.

But not yet. She felt a little lonely and looked forward to the date. Lab work was not enough.

She needed something else but had to be careful to avoid romanticizing, a fault. She exaggerated people's strengths, overlooked weaknesses, as she had with Greenberg. With Szaba she wouldn't make the same mistake, she thought, as she selected a conservative outfit, shamrock green gown that matched her eyes; not that she had many clothes to choose from. It didn't reveal too much but enough to show the contours of her body which, she hoped, Szaba would admire. Would she admire him? Time would tell; it always did.

And her? Had she been too hard on Noah? She could have let him sleep on the couch but he'd have been there for breakfast....Was she a misandrogynist? A hater of men? She feared she leaned in that direction and hoped Szaba would snap her out of it. If not? Maybe she was doomed to remain alone—a spinster, the worst that could happen except death or failure in the experiment.

CHAPTER 5

▼

He came in a silver limo.

Remembering his age, she climbed down when the buzzer rang. He inquired, rather formally, where she would care to dine. She was vaguely apprehensive, as though this was her first date.

They looked at each other, excitement in their eyes, Freddie was certain.

"I'm overdressed for the upper West Side."

He raised the cell phone, dialed a number he seemed to know by heart, asked for a table for two, rapped on the glass divider and told the chauffeur, "The Plaza." She noted the absence of "please". What did that signify? Poor comportment or an attempt to impress her with the unswerving loyalty of his minions?

In his mind, was she about to be among them? Freddie had better hold her own.

A small refrigerator, whiskey and glasses stood in a corner of the limo and he inquired if Freddie wanted a drink. "Fruit juice, please, Mr. Szaba."

"I'm Zygmunt. Ziggie or Zig to you. Wouldn't you prefer champagne?"

Champagne in a limousine? She reminded herself of Eloise at The Plaza. "Zig...." She couldn't suppress a smile. "Later, perhaps."

Her guard was up, however. She found herself a prisoner of memory, transported back to junior high school, when the boys had tried to neck. But Zig was an older man, past his prime, and she'd be safe with him, although his hotel name-dropping seemed pretentious.

Although she wasn't quite sure how a rich man should act. Perhaps he wasn't all that rich. Doubts surrounded her.

Before he'd squandered his wealth, her father, as she inescapably recalled, had hired limos and drivers for special occasions and she'd sat on his lap as a little girl. Szaba must be twice her age: she wouldn't sit on *his* lap for sure!

She'd never had much of a chance to be childish with Frederick but with Zig she felt comfortable and protected and that was the risk.

He asked innumerable questions as to her background and education, though his blunt tone made her suspect he already knew the answers. So many questions that she sensed herself exposed, open, translucent, while he remained walled off, distant, opaque. She'd become the child, he the paternal figure.

The chauffeur opened the door—he was stoop-shouldered and white-haired like an old family retainer. On Szaba's arm she climbed the short flight of steps to the entrance; his legs were as springy as hers. If she posted him, she imagined, his tissues wouldn't be gray but bright like his smile.

They were seated at a table by a window which overlooked horse-drawn carriages the smell of food floated in the air, near the wood-panelled Oak Bar and people greeted Szaba.

"You have lots of friends," she marveled.

He said congenially, "I could use more—I'm a solitary sort."

So was she, in fact.

"No wife?" He shook his head with vehemence. "Or girlfriend?"

"Not for the moment. As for friends, you lose them in business." Sadness entered his voice. "You have only associates or hangers-on."

"But at least people respect you."

"They only respect success."

"It seems to me you regard the world as hostile, Mr. Szaba. Excuse me, Zig."

She was aware he glanced at her breasts. Thank God the gown went to the neck.

"Not hostile so much as mean-spirited. They're only after profits."

"Aren't you?"

"I almost regard myself as performing a public service," Szaba said modestly.

"Almost?"

He sipped champagne and wiped his lips with a napkin. "Well, profits are not to be ignored."

"How about the philanthropy you spoke of?"

"Profits pay for that among other things."

"What kind of philanthropy?" she questioned.

"Research like yours."

"You don't expect a profit?"

"Helping to develop an anti-aging substance is a much more important goal."
She too sipped champagne. "But surely such a product would earn money."

Zig squinted. He had many mannerisms, as must she. Where did we learn such gestures? From our parents or were they inherited characteristics? "Who mentioned a product?"

It felt as though Freddie smiled only with her lipstick. An artificial smile: She was detached; money no longer interested her; she was content, living close to the poverty line as a single person. Science interested her more than anything, she believed. "You'd be fascinated by something that extends human life."

"You're young, Fredericka." He patted her hand.

"Freddie."

They'd finished the champagne—Freddie's sips had turned into more than a glass—she measured her intake as with the rodents in the lab. Zig suggested they move to the brocaded dining room where he ordered another bottle of Veuve Cliquot.

Freddie picked up the conversation where they'd left off. "What's young got to do with it?"

"Well, I wouldn't think growing old would be among your major concerns."

But it was. She too feared white hair and wrinkles, losing her precious bloom, coming to dust like Shakespeare's chimney sweepers. "I want the protein to stop people growing old."

"We'll soon learn," he said complacently.

The waiter brought leather-covered menus—prices had been omitted from hers. She couldn't help contrasting the elegant hotel with the Dominican joint where she and Noah had lunched and *she* had paid the bill!

"The protein works with the rats," she said. "I think such a product would be enormously popular...."

Zig gulped champagne and sneezed into a linen handkerchief that had been freshly laundered *and* pressed, Freddie noticed. He said with excitement. "A blockbuster!"

Freddie tried to accept his frame of reference—she was a scientist not a businessperson. To her amazement, she found the transition easy, and said, "Especially pegged to the fiftyish set. They tend to be affluent; they worry growing old will ruin their golf game; above all, they want to live! All this biotech news on the immortality of stem cells has raised their hopes. They believe scientific possibilities are limitless, that even death can be overcome."

His deep-set black eyes filled with admiration. "You're shrewd, darling."

Flustered, she said, "It's only an amateur opinion which you don't necessarily want." Or deserve, she thought.

"Your opinions interest me."

"I'm famished and getting slightly drunk."

Zig crooked a finger at the waiter. "Try the oysters. The filet mignon with sauce Béarnaise is exceptional. I'll have the same." They ordered and he bent forward. "If we ever reach that stage."

"I'm determined to."

The question is what to call the product."

"What name do you suggest?"

"Should I be talking to you?"

"You must. After all, I'll own the product."

"Okay. I now believe the rats will live three times as long as they were supposed to."

"A triple life expectancy?" Zig all but shouted. He calculated in his head. "The average human male in America lives to age 74. With the product he'd make it to 220."

"222, to be precise. But humans are different and you can't extrapolate our longevity from rodents," she said. "Even if we too ingest the protein."

"We need a brand name. You can't just ask for 'Protein X'."

"No."

"If only it conferred immortality."

"I wouldn't wish that on my worst enemy."

"Why?"

"It seems to me immortality—neotony. Forever young, to be precise—might be a dead end. I'm not joking. We wouldn't need to reproduce so our sex urge could dry up. Who wants to be a living fossil, as it were?"

"You must not speak out of hand. You don't know."

"I can surmise, for shit's sake."

"You needn't resort to profanity. You sound like a guttersnipe."

"Guttersnipe? Where did you learn such a word?"

"From my thesaurus."

"You use one?"

"I try to learn new words."

"'Immortality' might be a place to start."

"And end."

"Trouble is, 'Immortality' can't be abbreviated."

"'Forever' is shorter and so is 'always'…"

"As in 'to live forever' and 'always live'? But we couldn't claim that for the product. How do you convey the idea of a longer life span but *less than immortality*." Szaba took a gold fountain pen from the breast pocket of his tweed jacket. "How many 'm's' in immortality?"

"Two, for God's sake."

"You're certain?"

"Yes."

He drew boxes on the tablecloth and filled them with capital letters.

IMMORTALITY

He stared. "That won't work as a product name."

"Try again."

He crossed out an "M".

IMORTALITY

"Unattractive," she advised.

"Improve it, then."

"This is like Scrabble." She seized the fountain pen, inhaled, and deleted the "ITY" boxes.

""IMORTAL" with one "m" makes no sense."

"And we need something that suggests hi-tech," she said. "Like Teflon."

"From the rocket stuff?"

"Yes." She eagerly added "O N."

IMORTALON

"That ought to grab their fucking attention."

Zig hoisted his glass, "You are splendid."

"Hurray!"

"It seems perfect for a pharmaceutical product, though we'd need to test it with a focus group."

"The rats?" She bantered.

"I'll buy the tablecloth and frame it as a memento," Szaba said.

"Not a *momento mori* I trust," she said.

He ran fingers through his wavy gray hair. He was certainly good-looking for an older man, she thought. No, any man. Fatness made people seem old but he was slim, undoubtedly watched his weight and exercised, maybe with a trainer. Well-off people had advantages! The relative lack of lines on his face contributed to his aura of youthfulness but vigor was more important. Szaba had true charisma.

"Between us? Impossible, unless I'm too far over the hill for you."

Freddie was silent then said, "You have a few good years left, Zig," she said at last.

"How I wish. I have important things to do." Placing a hand on her arm, he gazed at the young woman.

She considered. Zig, though older, seemed kind and gentle and even more attractive because he came on slow, if he was coming on at all.

Lost in thought, she looked at him.

"Aren't you hungry?" Zig asked.

"I'd forgotten the food was here," she said, smelling filet mignon.

"Me too. It's like we were in another world."

"Sorry, we're stuck with this one, I guess.

The sound he made was meaningless. The moment of opportunity had opened and closed. She remained translucent and he opaque again, which conferred on him power over her. She refused yield.

They finished dinner, coffee and the champagne. He invited Freddie to his apartment at the Carlyle but, though tempted, she declined.

He brought her back to the upper West Side in the limo without a murmur of protest. On parting, they shook hands.

Upstairs she wondered what would have happened if she'd gone to bed with him. Perhaps he was just an old man with erectile dysfunction who couldn't penetrate and she'd have to have oral sex. But maybe he'd have proved robust and she would have been satisfied; well, chances were she'd never learn. She regretted that. Why couldn't she experiment with sex?

Freddie would give her undivided attention to the rat experiment unless fate intervened. And it always did, didn't it?

C H A P T E R 6

▼

The study rats' response to the protein was perfect—their noses wiggled as they sniffed the air for food and their eyes were bright. They seemed in remarkably good health with no indications of side effects. The controls, alas, had begun to show the ultimate side effect: death.

The only difference was the study rats' chow. Would the protein also work for larger creatures?

Now it was time to move up the evolutionary ladder to primates. The Animal Storage Unit delivered older beagles, a favorite lab animal because the breed could be standardized, and rhesus monkeys. Freddie could hardly bear the ruckus in the lab. All the animals sounded off as to let you know they were there.

She administered intravenous doses of the protein, though she had to use a cage squeezer with the monkeys—it jammed them against the bars—as a restraint. She felt fairly neutral toward the rodents (except when they had to be sacrificed) but for the rhesuses she had genuine affection. Their simian chatter and facial expressions reminded her of human adolescents. They became frantically active, rattling their cages and throwing their feces. The rhesus she'd named Monk, when she took it out of the cage, masturbated and ejaculated on her lab coat in a matter of seconds.

Suppose that happened with Szaba? Freddie pictured such an event in her mind. She laughed but tried to forget him, and failed. He kept recurring like a dream—a bad one? How would a psychoanalyst interpret that? Repulsion or attraction? She was thinking long-term, however. Perhaps she and Zig would last, assuming they began.

The short-term results with the protein were extraordinary. After several days the beagles no longer cowered. They made her think of retirement, partly a euphemism for withdrawal from society because of rejection by younger people. Perhaps Imortalon would create a new breed of oldsters who stood tall.

The animals' red blood cell, white blood cell and platelet counts were normal. Blood chemistries and liver functions were unchanged. Even in a rigid environment, which itself could cause dysfunction, the protein appeared efficient and without adverse effects.

Maybe a new age was about to begin, the age of Methuselah, with life-spans reaching almost to infinity.

Well, she wished this phase of the experiment would end but months would pass before they'd accumulated sufficient data to know if protein X inflicted harm. For now, at least, neither the canines nor the monkeys displayed the slightest loss of energy, despite their advanced years.

Christ, perhaps they'd succeed! Perhaps Imortalon, an odd name but no odder than that of many pharmaceutical products advertised on TV—would actually provide a "holiday from aging," maybe a slogan for the ads they'd need.

If protein X failed, all this effort would have been wasted. Lab science was strictly for suckers. Normal individuals need not apply.

Maybe she'd never been "normal". That dreadful skin condition, suddenly erupting at the strangest moments like a volcano, had haunted her since childhood and made her somewhat reclusive. Once, she'd taken refuge with horses her parents reared in New Jersey, though horses frightened her; she'd been thrown once. Since then, instead of riding she preferred to watch.

Yet horses soothed her too. She loved their graceful movements, their manner of swishing their tails. Their nature was gentle except when provoked and then they'd attack. Stay clear of angry horses! She'd been kicked.

The time came when her father could no longer afford the equines but she'd buy a few when she had the money.

Now, instead of horses, she watched the animals in her lab and preserved her countless observations in a black notebook, with numbered pages, issued by the hospital for experiments, to preserve data in an orderly format.

She kept the notebooks in a drawer, the most recent one on top. When she left the lab, she always carefully shut the drawer.

One day, on returning from lunch, she found the drawer slightly ajar.

Maybe she hadn't followed her own primitive security procedure. Yes, she'd forgotten. She had absolutely nothing to worry about. Except worry itself.

Still, she had to be on the alert and she plucked a blond hair painfully from her own head between the pages. When she came back the hair was gone. God!

Frantic, she went to Mulheran, who was aghast. "We're dealing with an invaluable pharmacobiological secret."

"Protein X," she said.

"We should have taken more serious precautions."

"Who would have dreamed of such a thing here at Columbia?" said she plaintively.

"Not I," Mulheran said and looked at her.

Freddie blamed herself. "I'm too trusting."

"Yes. You're young."

"When I'm older will I be more suspicious?"

"Probably. Experience teaches you that."

"Who wants that kind of experience?"

"It's more or less inevitable, Fredericka."

Alarmed, she told Geoff of a dark, burly man she'd seen in the corridor, near the copying machine.

"Lord." Mulheran crossed himself although he was an avowed atheist.

She realized disaster confronted them. All that effort might have served to benefit someone else! Others would possess the magical protein and reap the benefits, a nervously Freddie thought.

It was a dreadful time, she had to understand what happened.

"You need a special key to enter the lab. Not even Szaba has one."

"So who's the suspect? Martha? She might be stealing more than quarters."

"No. She took the same lunch break as I. If we eliminate Martha, that leaves Carlos."

"I've never trusted the chap. Is he, ah, homosexual?"

She thought of Carlos' curls. "How should I know, for heaven's sake? He seems a teeny bit effeminate but he might be androgynous. Or have a wife and kids. What's his sexuality got to do with it?"

"A homosexual might be blackmailed," Mulheran said ponderously.

"An old-fashioned idea. But he could have copied my notes."

"Yes."

"Have you applied for the patent?" Freddie asked.

Mulheran's pink cheeks turned red. "I haven't yet. I was waiting for...additional information."

Sure, she thought. Information from a bottle which tells you whether it's vodka or gin and what percentage of alcohol. Indispensable info for a heavy drinker.

"Why would he want the notes?" Freddie inquired. She could have beat herself for being naïve.

"To sell them," Mulheran said in a strangled voice.

"But how would he find a buyer?"

"He would only have to make a few inquiries. News travels fast in the biotech business. Did you cite the product name in your notes?"

"I referred to Protein X, as usual. The code word."

"Are you utterly certain?"

"Yes. No one has learned the name Imortalon from me."

*   *   *   *

Freddie woke the next morning determined to solve the mystery. Now she was in fact the lab detective and had to locate clues. If the worst had happened, the product idea had been stolen, just as Geoff's for an anti-cholesterol product, for money. Was nothing sacrosanct? Where had the concept of ethics gone?

Should she call the FBI? But the Feds would refuse to get involved. The same with the NYPD. It wasn't as though terrorists planned an attack. Industrial theft was the only charge that could be brought but who would prosecute? The WTO? Concerned with weighty matters like steel dumping, they'd laugh.

Okay. Perhaps she deserved the blame because of lax security but whodunit? she asked the animals who must have witnessed the crime, although they couldn't testify. Could a beagle take an oath?

The monkeys were gibbering as she proceeded with her routine, checking the supply of pellets and bottled spring water, carefully observing the rats—some were still kept on the side of the lab—the beagles, long-eared and brown, the rhesuses, for tell-tale signs of aging and, most important now, her associates as they performed their daily tasks.

What should she look for? she asked herself, spooning from a carton of yogurt. Something unusual…Martha's shiny new shoes? They might have been shop-lifted. Carlos' goatee had been shaved to sharpened point which, with his dark eyebrows, made him resemble the devil. Hmmmm.

He usually lunched in the lab from a paper bag—he seemed a creature of habit, like everyone—but that day took a call from his wife. Freddie, who answered the phone before passing it to Carlos, simply *assumed* the woman named Maria with a Spanish-flavored accent, was Carlos' wife. He wrote down things to get and she peeked at the list when he put down the phone: cough medicine, tissues....Somebody at home must have a cold.

Carlos went out hastily. Martha headed for the cafeteria and Freddie departed a few minutes later, wondering what would happen.

*   *   *   *

She couldn't deny she felt apprehensive and, looking uptown on Broadway, she saw Carlos emerge a low-priced drugstore carrying a plastic sack. He rubbed his chin beard—had he forgotten an item; was it a signal to an accomplice?—and went to a pay phone, inserted a coin and dialed. She watched for an eye blink or two, continued, then stopped at the corner, trapped by fear.

Then she lost track of Carlos in the crowd and decided her worries were fanciful. No, neurotic. The whole goddamned city was neurotic.

Or was her all-too vivid imagination responsible? Did Carlos *really* intend to sell the notes?

Maybe so. Maybe he had a drug habit. Or relatives to support in Latin-America. He could use the extra money. Yes. Undoubtedly, most of the Latino immigrants could.

She heard a siren and glanced as a police car, flashers on, pull to the curb, partially blocking traffic. Her attention was riveted when she heard the shrill song of an ambulance.

""POLICE LINE—DO NOT CROSS" said the yellow tape but she had an imperative to be there. She wasn't superstitious but felt whatever had occurred pertained directly to her, a shivery premonition.

A cop with stripes on his sleeve—he must have mistaken Freddie in her lab coat and trousers for a hospital physician—allowed her to cross the line.

Carlos—she knew instantly it was he from the Satanic beard—lay sprawled on the pavement. His body was twisted and she spotted a knife handle protruding from his back. His hands were empty.

"Is he dead?"

"Uh-huh," the cop said matter-of-factly.

"I can't help then."

She figured the police would quickly identify the corpse since Carlos' jacket had "COLUMBIA" stenciled on it and she called Mulheran from a nearby booth.

"Carlos has been murdered."

"Good God! What about the notes?"

"I didn't notice them," she shouted.

"Was there money on him?"

"I don't know. The cops will take inventory and give the dough to his wife."

"Maybe," was Mulheran's opinion.

Sobs convulsed her. She hated being so emotional but nothing could be done about it, except dig her fingernails into her palms.

And perspire. She always broke into a cold sweat when anxious.

She tried to reconstruct the crime. What exactly had she witnessed?

Freddie racked her brains. Finally, what had been a blur resolved itself into a faceless, heavy-set man crossing the street after Carlos had. Why had she noticed? Because the traffic light had been changing from yellow to red and in his rush he'd almost knocked an old woman down, she vividly recalled. The man hadn't bothered to help her up.

Maybe he was simply rude or perhaps he'd feared losing Carlos in the throng.

That had to be the case, she felt certain.

She'd actually seen a murderer.

So what? Homicide was a daily occurrence in New York.

But this instance was special. It involved a wonder drug that increased longevity, not hastened death.

Imortalon has claimed its first victim, she thought with foreboding. That was an important point. A fatality...

Perhaps she shouldn't continue work on the protein. It might be dangerous for her, like Szaba was, but defeating old age was the overriding objective.

*   *   *   *

That afternoon the brisk detectives came and asked about Carlos' job in Freddie's lab.

"He tested drugs on animals."

"Anything narcotic?"

"No, believe me."

"Did this guy have a locker?"

"In the basement."

"Show us."

They had a key from Carlos' pocket and opened the locker to inspect his meager possessions.

Among them was a copy of the U.S. Constitution.

So! Carlos had been studying for citizenship and if anyone had been watching the copier he or she had had the wrong impression. Carlos had been innocent of a biomedical caper.

Who had? No one, she thought. The strand of blond hair must have dropped to the bottom of the drawer.

Accidents happen…but homicide wasn't an accident.

*   *   *   *

To claim his belongings, the Latina widow arrived after the detectives had left. "Carlito won't have his father for his birthday," she sobbed. "Carlos always shaved to look like Satan to amuse the little one."

Freddie had to be absolutely certain. "Did Carlos call you from a phone booth before he was murdered?"

"Si. He wanted to know how much cough medicine to get."

Yes, Carlos had been innocent of a crime but somebody had stabbed him, believing he intended to sell precious secrets. Somebody who wouldn't take chances.

What would a buyer have learned about Protein X? That such a substance existed, that it prolonged life with lab animals.

But what if Carlos had also stolen a small quantity of protein X and was prepared to sell it? The secret would have been revealed.

Somebody, hypervigilant, could have a serious reason for concern. Somebody who didn't give a shit about human life, except maybe his or her own.

*   *   *   *

Mulheran denied repeating Freddie's suspicions of the stranger in the corridor, though maybe the prof didn't remember. He was foggy sometimes.

After the homicide, Szaba frequently dispatched a messenger for a copy of Freddie's notes, explaining he wanted to be up-to-date on the experiment. But, she suspected, he wanted absolute control. And it crossed her mind that Zig might somehow have been responsible for the murder. He wouldn't have stabbed Carlos himself, of course, but he might have sent a surrogate. However, he did send more orchids, with a card signed, "Love, Zig." Her image of Zig as kind and benevolent might require radical surgery.

Mulheran dismissed the killing as the result of a domestic dispute—the usual reason for murder among blacks and Hispanics. Besides, he had more important matters on His mind. What made Protein X work?

*   *   *   *

The aroma in Mulheran's lab next door to his office had changed over the years. His olfactory remembrance might have been misleading but it seemed to him, with the constantly changing chemicals he used, the smell never really became familiar. Today it was acrid, harsh, and unpleasant.

His work brought him into the far reaches of gene technology. He lived in a universe of blots, Southern blot (named for a Scottish research scientist whose first name he couldn't recall), represented the transfer of DNA from an agarose gel to a solid nitrocellulose, better known as nylon. The purpose was to fraction-ate (Mulheran strove to avoid obscure language but didn't entirely succeed) nucleic acids based on length and physical conformation. He looked for specific fragments and purified them.

The DNA migrated toward the north, attracted by North Pole magnetism and became the Northern blot, more visible under the electron microscope. (There was also a Western blot but Geoff would only need it in still more advanced research.)

The blots, all submicroscopic, were crucial tools in molecular biology for screening genetic diseases. Many genes had been linked to such diseases, like P53 to cancer.[1] Mulheran expected more linkages would be found.

Preparing the electron microscope—weighing and measuring particles—occu-pied much of the day and it was mid-afternoon before he had cloned from the DNA Greenberg had supplied. He now had an inkling as to the nature of Protein X. One of the substances he identified was the Fibroblast Growth Factor.

Mulheran believed FGF-1, as he labeled the substance, "acted as a barrier to the genes responsible for human aging."

He spoke aloud, as if practicing for a lecture, and failed to hear Freddie as she entered on silent feet. "How?" she said.

"You startled me, Fredericka!"

"Go on, prof."

------

1. The complete gene complement of man comprises about 3 billion pairs, or 50,000 to 100,000 genes contained in over 200 types of cells, each with its own function.

"This Fibroblast Growth Factor contains 159 amino acids. Among other things, it helps repair tissue damage by forming new vasculature blood vessels. It has an effect on primitive stem cells…"

"The basis of our organs," she added.

"Uh-huh. We can speculate that it would be possible to grow new hearts, livers and so forth, by means of stem cells and the right protein. At any rate, the FGF-1 apparently carries a blueprint that could restore the body to the best possible condition."

"Sensational!"

"And it might prolong life."

"Why?"

"Why?" Mulheran paused, as if to gather his thoughts. "The potent hematopoietic cytokine is actually found in the brain. So far it has been largely ignored but might bring about, ah, younging."

"Younging?"

"The obverse of aging, of course. In much larger and possibly toxic quantities it could dewrinkle the skin. Imagine 20-year-old skin on a 60-year-old! The elasticity, color and underlying tissue structure would be as with a young person."

"That could eliminate the need for plastic surgeons."

"Yes."

Molecular physicists weren't given to excitement but Mulheran could scarcely disguise his. The watery blue eyes sparkled. "And I should add, those irritating things from poor bladder control to hemorrhoids might disappear."

"Don't be gross, prof."

"What's gross where the body's concerned?"

"Besides diseases? Aging, perhaps."

"You make aging sound nefarious, Fredericka."

"It's sort of like a thief in the night—steals youth."

Until then she hadn't understood how personal the anti-aging protein had become for her. She wanted Imortalon to defeat old age and free mankind from its clutches, a transformation. Let the good times roll!

The prof droned on…"and more serious physiological problems might vanish. This is only theory, mind you, but FGF-1 might stop aging in its tracks."

"Our protein contains the growth factor?"

"Why else would I be interested? It might mean artificial joints would no longer be required. Protein X would eventually grow new bones and cartilage to replace them. Or they may self-repair instead of self-destruct as in so many autoimmune diseases like arthritis, MS and Parkinson's. Those who hobble might throw away their crutches and run in marathons, though we're a long way from that technologically." The professor spoke with a jocular solemnity and it was hard to know if he intended to be humorous.

"So the aging body might remain more youthful throughout?"

"No reason why not. FGF-1 elixir could revolutionize geriatric medicine."

"Elixir?"

"Think of it as a survival cocktail of the growth factor."

"Goodbye to old age homes because of Protein X. With no side effects."

"That remains to be seen," Mulheran said. "And a lot more, too. We haven't considered the demographic implications and repercussions. People are already living considerably longer—life expectancy will reach 79.3 years by the year 2030, the Social Security Administration predicts; some say higher, but with Protein X the older groups could skyrocket. Why, you could have more oldsters than youngsters! And senior citizens would have the votes. That's what I'm afraid of, a gerontocracy."

"Rule by the ancients, huh?"

"For instance, they could raise the legal age for imbibing alcohol."

"Have you had a drink, prof?"

"I'm not old enough!" Mulheran said with a snort.

"Don't kid around, prof," Freddie said. "An enormous normal life span could be a bummer."

"Bummer?"

"A real bad trip."

Mulheran adjusted his glasses. "I suppose."

"Are we on the same wavelength, prof?"

"You mean memory?"

"Memory loss."

Mulheran nodded. "Hard enough to remember what happened to you last year, much less a decade ago."

"Many decades for people using Imortalon. Even centuries if life expectancy rises above 200 years."

"You'd need appointment books to check on what you forgot. The second half of your life would be occupied by trying to recall the first."

"You'd require a computer to keep track of whom you'd been to bed with. Not me, of course."

Freddie reflected. If she could relive her life, would she have made different choices? On balance she didn't believe so except for the rash.

"Nor I," Mulheran said sadly.

She giggled. "One could forget one's own promiscuity."

"And almost everything else."

"Oblivion isn't attractive. Maybe we shouldn't interfere with Mother Nature," Freddie said.

"We must."

"Why?"

"Think of technology as an Everest. The identical reason Mallory only half-joking gave for climbing the mountain—because it's there."

Freddie imagined Geoff's bald dome as the top of Everest and his fringe of white hair as snow. She suddenly felt a chill. He kept the temperature low in his lab, right?

*   *   *   *

After Freddie had gone, Mulheran sat at the bench. He had to wonder if the younging effect would be permanent or taper off, so that the protein would become ineffective and people who thought they'd been granted a respite from old age would suddenly plunge into the grave. What a travesty that would be! And they might not know until Imortalon had been on the market for many years.

Hearts that had been beating briskly would begin to slow. Those who'd ceased making payments on burial plots would be desperate. Those who'd canceled their orders for gravestones would hurriedly renew them. The situation might resemble that Himalayan Buddhist sanctuary Freddie had talked about (he couldn't remember the title, (a work of fiction, she'd said) where the promise of eternal life proved a cruel illusion if worshippers departed from the premises—stopped taking Imortalon.

Five o'clock, his usual drinking hour, had passed and Mulheran reached for the flask in which he disguised the vodka when a timid knocking sounded at the door. Had Fredericka returned? "Come in," Mulheran said.

He tried to place the woman who entered. Martha, wasn't it? "What do you want, Martha?" he said, barely able to hide his irritability. He'd never seen her in street clothes.

"You needn't be rude, Professor."

"That wasn't my intention," he said with as much graciousness as he could muster. His mind was on the flask.

"It sure smells strange in here."

"I'm accustomed to the odor," he said and waited. Martha said nothing so he asked, "Problems in the lab?"

Martha uttered a rueful laugh. "Without Carlos I get lonely and Freddie gives too many orders."

"Isn't Fredericka there?"

"She rushed out to spend a weekend at her father's." Martha shifted her feet. "I thought you might be lonely too."

Geoff stroked his bald head and scanned the woman with eyes still blurry from using the electron microscope. She wasn't exactly as they said, a looker; thick ankles, wide waist, drooping boobs, a double chin, pouches…but, considering her age, she wasn't bad dressed up. He found himself tempted to invite her for dinner—as usual he had no plans—but couldn't quite summon the nerve. And, he had vodka for companionship. At last he responded.

"I'm not."

"Not…?"

"Lonely."

"Perhaps you should know more about me." Her voice quavered.

"What's to know?"

✳   ✳   ✳   ✳

Martha wasn't certain how much of her past she should give him. That she'd been abandoned as an infant and raised in an orphanage? That she'd almost been expelled from school for truancy? That she'd hung around with a tough crowd? That she'd pulled herself together enough to graduate from a junior college? Mulheran wouldn't be interested in such stuff. Too ordinary.

"I was a buyer at an expensive department store. I made gobs of money but…"

"But?"

"I couldn't resist taking the things home and, because, well…"

"Go on."

"I don't remember which came first—thievery or addiction. I sold the stuff to pay for heroin." She rolled up her sleeve, conscious of showing him needle marks.

✳   ✳   ✳   ✳

Martha knew Mulheran would be appalled.

For scientists like him, narcotics were a taboo: they could be easily obtained or, if necessary, concocted in a lab, but to swallow, inject or sniff hard drugs was inconceivable. Narcotic abuse represented an intellectual line he could not and would not cross. He felt both pity and contempt toward those who had.

"You're off the stuff?"

"I promise. After I was fired they put me into a methadone program and it worked. I'm drug-free."

Mulheran thought of the loose change episode. He said with scorn, "Have you rid yourself of *all* your bad habits?"

"Just about. I have little left to live for, though—no husband, no kids, no boy-friend." She gazed at him imploringly.

"What am I, your father confessor?" Mulheran snapped.

"Are you Catholic?"

"Of course not. I'm proud to be an atheist."

"Tell me more, please. I'm here. I'm listening."

Geoff suddenly wanted to open up. He had nobody to converse with except about science and that subject was all too familiar. He needed to reveal himself on a personal level. Why not? Martha had set an example.

"I was married…," he began.

"I know. Not happily, I assume."

"She played around with my colleagues, made me look like a fool."

"Why did you think she was unfaithful?"

"Because, on leaving the shower, she concealed her breasts and she wasn't modest. She had to be covering up because she had someone else."

"How did you react?"

"I considered suicide but to kill yourself requires more courage than I pos-sessed at the time."

"And now?"

"I consider suicide much less often."

"You prefer to die slowly?"

Mulheran blinked. It wasn't as though he'd signed a contract with death…he could still choose not to die. What would be the correct decision. Whose embrace would he prefer, a woman's or the Grim Reaper's. He shivered—the lab was cold. A woman would warm him.

But he'd talked too much. Martha worked at the hospital. "That's enough."

"No. All the more reason I should take care of you." She placed an affectionate hand on his.

Geoff hesitated—he would have enjoyed a woman in his bed—but withdrew his fingers. "Thanks. I don't need taking care of and I'm far too busy for a rela-tionship."

"Listen! I'm an ex-addict," she cried out, "and if I broke with heroin…I know you drink to excess. You start to mumble in the late afternoons. That must be when you start drinking. Right?"

"Well…." Geoff glanced at the flask.

"I'll help you stop. You're lonely too, I'm willing to bet."

"You won't find a reference to loneliness in the theoretical scientific literature," Geoff said defensively. "It's not our concern."

"Science isn't everything. There's also love." She tilted her face, as if offering a kiss.

"Love will have to wait," he said.

"Love isn't a solid. It's more like a vapor. Wait too long and the vapor disappears," Martha said pleadingly.

He backed off from her as though she carried an awful disease and was thus a threat to his very existence. "Calm yourself," he begged.

"Calm? I don't wish to be calm. Can't you tell I'm making a declaration of…." Martha's lower lip trembled and she ceased to speak.

Geoff said, "I think you're angry."

"Angry? Sure I'm angry. At being rejected."

"You're not being rejected—exactly."

"Feels like it."

"The timing isn't right, that's all."

"Okay," she challenged. "When is, then?"

"After I'm convinced the protein has no side effects."

"Which might be months!"

"I need to concentrate." A shadow crossed his features as he walked to the window, staring bleakly into the darkness.

Martha's frumpish face crumpled like a rose, and she departed.

I must sleep with Martha before it's too late, he thought.

Geoff poured himself high-proof vodka—alcohol was a stimulant before one became sodden. He began to write quickly on a legal pad: "Protein X is a polypeptide, unique in size and structure, a highly active compound. I've seen nothing similar these many years. It may extend life but in what fashion? Would we be contented creatures or something grotesque?

He refilled the flask with vodka and tried to restrain himself to tiny sips. "Only Nature can provide the answer but why should she? In a sense, this application of molecular physics is beyond Nature. It is the work of man and we don't understand the potential for…mischief, evil…"

Nothing bad will happen, he told himself. That trouble waits for the traveler on the road to success is merely an old wives' tale and scientists aren't superstitious.

Again Geoff crossed himself. He thought, if I get into a jam with the monkey virus—did I check every last footnote?—Martha will be sympathetic. Maybe she'll offer a helping hand.

He wondered again, did I *really* check the footnotes completely?

What if I didn't? Would there be a disaster? And for whom? Me, perhaps.

CHAPTER 7

▼

Freddie had expected a smooth trip ahead and why not? The study group animals were in excellent shape and the experiment's success seemed virtually certain, she told Szaba.

"*Virtually?*" He seemed to shake the word as a dog would a bone. "Don't count on that."

Columbia was the flagship of New York's teaching hospitals and an experiment that employed a large number of live animals raised questions as to the purpose. It proved impossible to elude the hospital's bureaucracy or the Animal Rights Committee.

"Listen," said a gaunt doctor, a vice-president, "our institution doesn't engage in commercial research. We're only concerned with pure science."

Freddie answered, "How do you define pure? Science is based on the hypothetical and making money from this research is strictly hypothetical. We're trying to prove the usefulness of a protein and the tests might fail."

"But if the experiment succeeds?"

"The Prof might win a Nobel Prize for science," Freddie said hotly.

"The hospital must share in the proceeds from the experiment," said the vice-president.

"So talk to *him*."

The veep did, Freddie learned, and Geoff persuaded him FGF-1, combined with an unspecified protein, might some day revolutionize medicine, but not yet.

Her approach was pragmatic. The big pharmaceutical outfits—like Pfizer, Merck and Roche—spent billions in research and discovery. Many products didn't show efficacy or were abandoned because the drug lacked a market or sizeable market share, had too many competitors or couldn't garner FDA approval. The research they spent money on justified their steep prices, they said. Otherwise, their stockholders would complain.

But Szaba lacked enormous funds from previous products—in short a reliable income. The fate of Imortalon could be like a rodent's, about to be sacrificed.

Freddie had misled the vice-president. Far from being bleak, experimental results thus far had been encouraging. The study group of rodents still hadn't aged and the beagles and monkeys remained fine, with no apparent toxic effects. All signs pointed to the conclusion that Imortalon would be effective.

She said to Martha, "People will enjoy living longer in excellent health. They'll look forward to spending extra Thanksgivings and Christmases with their grandchildren and great-grandchildren."

Martha grumbled, "What about women like me who don't even have children?"

"There's more to life than kids."

"Someone to share your bed with? But I've always slept alone."

"Haven't you always hoped you'd find a mate?"

Martha sighed, "I suppose."

"The protein would buy you more time to achieve your goal. The same must be true for those who want to write the perfect poem or paint a masterpiece."

"Well, I believed Prof Mulheran would be a suitable partner but he turned me down, I think."

"And I think Geoff's a goddam lush."

"Uh-huh."

"The bottle's more important to him than a woman could be. Don't take it to heart."

"But I have to—we die too soon. It isn't fair but that's how things are."

"How things *were*," Freddie said, watching the old rhesuses swing on their cage bars. The beagles ran on treadmills, panting like little long-distance runners. "The protein will change things magically."

"The drug—I assume that's the objective—might be too costly for folks like me," Martha pointed out. "Suppose Medicare and the HMO's refuse to pay for it?"

"People would demand the product as a human right, as men did with Viagra and Levitra."

"Maybe there *won't* be a product," Martha announced curtly. "The students are up in arms against the experiment."

*   *   *   *

Martha always lunched in the cafeteria and had heard rumors that originated among the medical students. English scientists had cloned a sheep from genetic material and goats had been cloned as well. What next? A horse? they asked. Or a cow with a dog's head created by genetic manipulation? Instead of mooing, the cowdog would yap incessantly.

TV news shows called Mulheran and asked to send reporters and camera crews. The prof, amused, directed them to the Bronx where they'd find the zoo-morph.

What had started as a prank became serious when the gaunt V.P. and several faculty members asked to inspect the lab and put the rumors to rest.

Freddie tried to smile. "You really believe we'd engage in genetic manipulation? That I'd clone a monster?"

"God knows what you're up to," said the veep. "You've used hundreds of rodents. Do you cook them for breakfast?"

"You're subjecting me to harassment," Freddie yelled at the vice-president. "You intend to get me out of here, huh? Well, we won't budge. Professor Mulheran will protect us."

But, hovering over the old-young primates as if she were their mother, she let them in, along with a nurse who introduced herself as Felicia Nay.

The RN seemed surprised on seeing beagles riding bikes, shocked when Monk ejaculated on her uniform. "Messy," she objected.

"No more messy than spit," Freddie said.

"I don't like being spat at either," Nay said primly.

"At least the animals aren't monsters," Freddie said.

When the unwelcome visitors had gone, Martha remarked, "Sooner or later we'll have to relocate."

*   *   *   *

Among the major traumas, right up there with a death in the family, sickness and divorce, is moving. The prospect of needing a different lab gave Freddie a severe anxiety attack: she couldn't sleep; she spoke faster; she felt like crying but she refused to surrender to tears.

She was more stressed out than she'd ever been even after the one-night stand when she'd contemplated an abortion. The pregnancy had proved a false alarm.

She'd been sorry in a way, might have enjoyed an infant, because she lacked/ didn't want a husband. Anyhow, parenthood wasn't for her.

Now, for some reason, she thought of Noah, skulking in Cold Spring Harbor. He wouldn't set foot in the city, which he claimed he didn't like. But of course he feared Freddie didn't like him which wasn't quite true. In fact, she missed Noah in an obscure corner of her heart but remained suspicious of his motives.

Maybe a facial would relax her.

A Dominican beauty parlor down the block gave them. It was not far from the spot where Carlos had been stabbed and she remembered the blood had the notes been stolen? She was now convinced there had been no notes.

A woman gently kneaded her cheek with a fragrant lotion but her fingers drew back. "*Que es?*"

"What?" Freddie asked.

"*Como un pescado.*"

"A fish? Hand me a mirror."

She'd given herself a cursory glance in the mirror that morning and her cheeks had been smooth. Now, with bewildering speed, exacerbated no doubt by stress, the rash had emerged, an ugly bluish welt like fish scales, and hard. It was tiny but would spread, she knew.

She couldn't bear to look at herself; at the hospital they'd joke that she'd been cloned from a fish.

"Give me makeup, *maquillaje, mucho maquillaje.*"

The woman applied pancake and, before Freddie could object, eye shadow, mascara, lipstick.

Freddie inspected herself in the mirror. She looked like a whore though you couldn't see the rash. Still she'd never be certain it wouldn't burst out from under the pancake.

On the street she wiped off the eye shadow and mascara but left on the pancake; still, she avoided people as much as possible. As early as she could, she went back to her apartment and stayed there alone.

The rash was spreading and the antibiotic a hospital doctor prescribed failed to help.

She refused to see a soul except at work.

She disliked being solitary, as if she were in prison, but felt she had no choice.

She hated ugliness.

Herself.

Nearly as bad as a rash, vanity had been a problem her whole adult life she thought, and she tried to suppress. If she stopped going to the lab, how could she continue the experiment? She forced herself to coax Greenberg.

But she coaxed Greenberg into having a meal in the city. He told her the ichtyosis didn't matter—he was falling in love with Freddie, "despite the skin condition".

She had to ask herself if Noah was being honest. Why couldn't she bring herself to trust him? He seemed too nice.

"Beauty is skin-deep, huh? But blemishes go to the bone," she said bitterly.

"An awful adage. To me you're radiant."

"Like a goddam light bulb? Well, I need a shade!"

"Don't knock yourself. Put your shoulders back."

She couldn't accept his simple advice. "Do I sound like a narcissist?"

"Maybe. A Stoic would be preferable. That implies courage. Don't surrender to a rash."

"I'm hideous, can't you tell?"

"Not through the veil." She had purchased a cheap cotton veil held on with an elastic band. "You look like you're in purdah."

"How am I to eat?"

"Well, Muslim women aren't supposed to eat in public with men."

She pushed aside the veil and grimaced. "I can't stand people."

"Even men?"

"Especially men. They stare at you."

"Women don't?"

"In a different way."

"Maybe you could."

"The fact is, my cheek is disgusting."

"Forget it,"

"Haven't you noticed? I'm depressed."

"You're much too moody."

"My privilege. Women are twice as likely to become depressed as men. Gender is destiny."

"Oh yeah? We both have our problems. Stop rubbing your cheek for God's sake. You'll make a habit of it. Quit bitching and eat your meal. Sooner or later the rash will vanish."

*   *   *   *

Martha had a sore throat and Freddie fed the animals in her absence. She'd unlatched the cages and was measuring the protein when Monk suddenly jumped on her shoulder, jarring her arm.

The protein spilled on one of her double latex gloves. She scraped it into the vial, tossed the little rhesus into the cage with a quick caress. She continued feeding the critters.

Feeding frenzy was more like it. How they ate! They would have consumed twice as much protein as they'd been given, and yet they didn't gain weight. Thinking of a diet product, she must have rubbed her cheek.

In hours the ichthyosis disappeared and with it the mild depression. "Sooner or later the rash will vanish," Noah had predicted and it had. She must have developed resistance. Antibodies....

*   *   *   *

During her brief isolation Freddie had forbidden Szaba to visit and his silent inducement, she figured, was to tell Mulheran to increase her salary, though Zig wrote the checks.

"Thank you," she said to Geoff.

"A gesture of appreciation really, for doing a tremendous job. It's a pittance."

"But enough to buy a couple of horses. I've wanted them for quite awhile."

"Where will you keep them?" Geoff asked.

"At my father's place in New Jersey. He'll board them for me and won't charge me a cent."

When he'd been flush, Frederick had owned a sizeable parcel of land near Short Hills, fox hunting country. He'd leased the acres to a farmer who grew crops. After Freddie's mother's death, he'd sold off most of the land, which eventually became a fancy shopping center. If her father had held on, he would have been a millionaire, Freddie pointed out unkindly.

"Woulda—shoulda—you can't relive the past. I don't care about big bucks."

Freddie understood why she held serious money in contempt—she'd inherited the attitude from her dad. "I agree."

"More enjoyable to wander on the boardwalk, smelling the ocean breezes."

"At least that must be healthy."

"And then I return to the small-stakes poker tables."

"Where there's second-hand cigarette smoke. Why do you like gambling so much, Dad?"

"Hard to explain. It's a tiny world where nothing is predictable."

"You find that exciting?"

"I don't look for excitement, just winning against the other players."

"Competition?"

"Oh yes."

"But you weren't very competitive when you were in business."

"Gambling is cleaner. A matter of odds."

"Beating them?"

"You can't beat the odds. Understanding them mathematically is all you can hope for."

"I should think a computer could do that for you."

"It can. The younger players use computers to refine the odds."

"Don't they always win?"

He smiled benignly. "A computer can't teach you when to bluff. Besides, some of us older players seem to have computers in our brains. And we manage our emotions better than younger folks. In gambling one's age doesn't matter, a major reason I enjoy it."

*   *   *   *

She'd take a chance with older equines.

At an auction, Freddie purchased three cheap, aged horses, two mares and a stallion. Normally, they grazed in the fields but it was winter now and she had to supplement their diet.

Ever curious, she mixed the protein—the price from the supplier had fallen from $8000 a gram to nearly nothing, they'd bought so much—with oats her father gave them. The next weekend she visited, the nags seemed friskier, their coats more shiny. Why, the stallion on his ancient legs even tried to mount the mare! When she whistled to call them, two fingers between her lips, they trotted to her instantly. No sign of hearing impairment or reduced energy. And, in human terms, they must have been superannuated.

What did we mean by aging? A fixed condition or a variable? Something you could affect by force of will? A matter of spirit?

Perhaps her imagination played tricks but the equines actually seemed younger than they had been.

*   *   *   *

She said to Mulheran, "Were you serious when you spoke of younging?"

"Not really. It was speculation, that's all."

"But could Protein X reverse aging?"

"Possibly. Though I doubt it. I get carried away by my theories, thrilled, if you will. I tend to exaggerate, a fault I accept. I can't change, but on sober reflection, I don't believe the laws of nature can be repealed."

"Why the hell not? We're at the forefront of science." She raised her voice.

"Pot bellies won't disappear or poor circulation either. They claim to have a cure for baldness but I wonder if a pill can produce a full head of hair?" Like a jocular friar, Mulheran laughingly rubbed his pinkly gleaming pate. "With the protein, we can stem the tide, that's all."

"Delay aging. But what if Protein X possesses a kind of magic?"

"The magic protein," Geoff murmured.

"Suppose it causes you behave youthfully?"

"Any proof of that, Fredericka?"

Unlike the lab animals the horses hadn't lived under controlled conditions and an experiment had to be repeatable by other scientists to gain validity (they'd commissioned backup studies at another lab) which was why she hadn't mentioned the equines. Nor had she thought to measure the protein her father sprinkled on the oats. "No," she said.

"Why did you bring up the subject then?"

"Because…" she paused. "If I took the protein I'd hope it would restore my memories of girlhood. Fantasies help keep us youthful."

"Older people have fantasies too, Fredericka," Mulheran said.

"Regarding sex, I suppose."

"That, and being rich."

Freddie was begun to agree with the rich part. Was she a mercenary?

*   *   *   *

As a child, she remembered she'd fantasized—her mother restored to health, her father demonstrating genuine affection. But he was inexorably tied to his wife and even when Freddie sat on his lap in the rented limo, she knew her dad's thoughts were with her slowly-dying mother. Freddie had resented that, being too young to understand.

Something in her father's soul eluded her. Something she couldn't quite artic-ulate. As though he tried to achieve a certain peace, albeit on a remote level, while she seemed doomed to eternal striving.

Even now, she disliked Frederick's low-key passion for gambling, not merely because he was wasting his life and squandered money (although he didn't lose much, or even held his own at the tables but because she still yearned for his affection.

How could she get it? If only she could accept Frederick for what he was: a gambling bum.

"Dad," she'd say, eyeing Frederick's ancient Cadillac which he constantly pol-ished, "why can't you stay away from Atlantic City? Why can't you settle down, meet a new woman, remarry?" But he never would. For the remainder of his existence he'd continue to worship Freddie's mother, as if she were a shrine.

Freddie resented that her father paid more attention to her mother's money than to her. It was a major reason she cooperated with Szaba.

Flowers frequently surrounded her mother's photograph on his chest of draw-ers. It was as though he prayed there. Atlantic City represented escape from grief, Freddie guessed. Again, she urged Frederick to give it up.

"Can't you stop trying to change me?" he said.

"No!"

"Well, I'm a rock, sort of."

"A rock?"

"The kind of poker player who can't be bluffed when he likes his hand. If he won't fold, you should."

What was he saying? That she meddled too much with his life? Did Freddie do the same with Zig and Noah? Could <u>she</u> change? Or was she a rock?

Sort of, Freddie supposed.

*   *   *   *

"No," she said again and again to Zig in response to his entreaties for a date.

He seemed undisturbed, as though she'd eventually surrender. He had Euro-pean charm, slick and old-worldly, on his side of the equation.

"You're a 'no' machine," he said.

"Sometimes I say 'yes'."

Indeed, she asked herself why there had been so few men in her life. A lot of guys had asked her out but almost always she'd declined, pleading exams, a headache, work at the hospital and other excuses. As she'd hinted to Noah, Freddie was shy, not that her quintessential timidity appeared on the surface.

She'd made a serious effort to find a nice guy but none really suited her so in the end it had come down to two men who claimed they adored her. Eventually she'd have to choose.

Zig was saying, "What concerns me is Greenberg. I suspect you're stringing the fellow along. It's me you want, not him."

"If that's not arrogant it's pretty close." She laughed nervously, conscious of her charm.

"A difference exists between arrogance and confidence, that is, pride, which is usually not deserved, and confidence, usually based on fact. I'm confident I'll get you."

"What makes you so sure?" she asked.

"This Greenberg's a loser," Zig said flatly.

"You haven't even met him!"

"I don't need to." He was dropping the courtly mask, revealing a ruthless man.

"Because he hasn't suspected we might make a bundle with the protein?"

"In part. And that I feel love for you."

"Lust is more like it."

She thought about Greenberg. His persona lacked edge but he compensated with bravery. Freddie found herself perplexed.

Why did Szaba attract her? Was she seeking fatherly love? When he spread his arms to offer an embrace, he reminded her of Dracula, maybe because of his shiny teeth (he'd had the dental implants), yet she shied away, skittish as one of her horses. It was all Frederick's fault for rejecting her.

Really? Didn't women experience lust just like men? A burning sensation in the groin? Desire?

Yes. Completeness.

She tired of being a closed book. The cover must be opened to herself above all.

What secret did she have? She was a person who enjoyed pain—a masochist? Yes, that would explain lots of things: her relationship with her father, with Zig and Noah, even Mulheran and the attempt to forestall death, probably doomed to failure, who desires that?

But for the moment she'd exercise restraint. The volume must remain shut. "Tell you what. Let's wait."

"Until?"

"We have something to celebrate."

As Mulheran had suggested, perseverance was key to science. Almost a year had passed since she'd begun to experiment with Protein X, met Greenberg and Szaba. Between the two she vacillated, liking Noah's gentleness but drawn to the power Zig seemed to exude.

PART II

▼

HUMAN TESTING

CHAPTER 8

▼

Almost a year sped by and Freddie paused to review earlier rat tests: no observed pathology, even with a high dose of the protein.

The long-term studies on the dogs and simians, almost complete, substantiated the rodent findings. In testing, she'd expected negative events, such as elevation of liver enzymes or slowing motility of the gut, factors related to aging, but none had appeared.

Phase I human testing could commence while the animal studies were under way, just so the stability of the protein compound had been fully explored, Freddie learned from an informal telephone chat with an FDA safety officer.

Mulheran assured her he'd kept samples of the substance to be sure it didn't destabilize under a wide range of conditions.

"We have a green light, chemically speaking," Geoff said.

"But not from Noah. He discovered the magic protein. He ought to be informed now," Freddie said.

The Prof shook his bald head emphatically. "I now hold the patent. He hasn't the faintest idea the new protein has a practical application unless you told him."

"I haven't."

"Good. We're dealing with a pharmaceutical secret, maybe worth billions which Greenberg might reveal."

The codger could be tough. He increasingly displayed avarice, having been financially insecure for so long. Being on *The Journal of Molecular Biology*'s list of world-class scientists hadn't assuaged his desire to be wealthy. He wanted a slice of the proverbial pie, proving to Freddie Americans couldn't resist the lure of money.

And they never would. When the NASDAQ hit 15,000, they'd be expecting double that number. Americans were out to own the world.

Except her. She had no stocks or bonds and hardly any money in the bank. Her needs were excruciatingly simple. Her credo had always been not to own more possessions than she could jump over, and that was mostly true (except for the couch and the chest of drawers). She spurned a car (she took the train to Short Hills) and had only a small wardrobe of inexpensive clothes. She borrowed books from the library, got workouts from lifting weights, and using the stationery bike, climbing stairs to her apartment and running to and from the lab. She'd never gain weight—her metabolism was perfect and she refused to overeat. Her stereo and artwork weren't worth hanging onto; her most important possession was the single bed she slept in. She considered herself generous and fair-minded.

That Noah receive his due preoccupied her but Szaba, unsurprisingly, agreed with Mulheran, she learned when she finally accepted his invitation—Freddie had been stubborn, perhaps *too* stubborn—and he picked her up in the silver limo. "Greenberg doesn't deserve to be part of the action? Is that what you mean? You're unspeakably egotistic, Zig."

"No, practical. Potential deals might collapse if he blabbed. Everyone would be claiming the protein."

"Still, for God's sake, he deserves something." Freddie felt honor-bound to protect Greenberg, even though she preferring Szaba. She hoped Noah would find someone else, although like her Dad he seemed to be the kind of man who fell in love with only one woman for his whole life.

"Why? He's in the dark as to what he discovered and must remain so. Perhaps, down the line, we'll offer him a stipend. As a legal formality, of course. Not that we must."

"What about Cold Spring Harbor lab?"

"As scientists will, Greenberg was undoubtedly moonlighting. He developed the protein in his spare time. The lab would have no claim either."

Maybe she ought not to have given in so easily but Freddie was powerless and abandoned the effort. "Where are we headed? The Plaza?"

"To my private hell," Szaba said.

They went to the Carlyle where Zig showed off his luxurious apartment. Freddie counted nine rooms, excluding the servant's quarters. "Do you own the place?"

"I pay an exorbitant rent with an option to buy. If Imortalon hits perhaps I will, though the apartment will cost a bloody fortune."

"Whose blood?"

"The stockholders of other companies I've been involved with. Excuse me."

He retired to his massive bedroom and emerged in a paisley smoking jacket. The maid had relieved Freddie of her old topcoat—it was fall and chilly—and she wore a simple dress that she'd possessed since college. The maid in a starched uniform served hors d'oeuvres in the living room—sliced salmon with toast, caviar with crackers, ham with a dollop of goat cheese embedded.

"*Bavarian* ham, *French chèvre*—the California brand is awful—*Scotch* salmon, the best, and *Russian* black caviar," Zig said with emphasis, as he uncorked the Veuve Cliquot. He raised his crystal glass. "Cheers.

"For?"

"Completing the animal studies and to human testing which is about to start."

"We still require FDA approval every step of the way."

"A snap, believe me."

"We have to submit an IND application."

"Investigational New Drug. I know the drill," Szaba said.

And did he understand the risks of submitting fraudulent data to the FDA? Surely Szaba wouldn't take chances with his money by tinkering with the protocols, but just the same, she felt apprehensive. She said, "The application must specify, among other things, the age group the product will be targeted for. Between 55 and 70 years old, Professor Mulheran and I have concluded."

"Must you be quite that precise?" Szaba said with a sigh of frustration.

"We're aware from the animal studies the protein would be wasted on individuals older than that—aging is already too pronounced...."

Szaba interrupted, "I wish people of truly advanced years would use the drug. We'd have a far larger market. Can't you fudge the protocol a little?" Zig clipped a Cuban cigar, applied flame from the Tiffany table lighter and inhaled.

"Younger people will mob doctors for Imortalon prescriptions as they did with Prozac before they started worrying about neurological effects. You mustn't be avaricious."

"Avar...."

"Greedy."

"And you *mustn't* lecture me," he threatened, reminding her again of her dad.

Freddie spooned caviar over a cracker and added bits of cooked egg white. "Somebody should," she said.

"But I won't listen. I intend to be rich, very rich."

"Very-very? Like a Saudi prince?" she teased.

Szaba smiled.

"Aren't you rich now?"

Szaba frowned. "I am in a way but I owe a wad to my backers."

"You've lost money then?"

Szaba shrugged. "Some years. It's a matter of luck."

"May I have more champagne?"

The maid poured. "When I first met you I almost had to force champagne down your beautiful throat."

"Not any longer. I love champagne, I've decided. Who are your backers?"

"East Europeans. Poles from Warsaw mostly. My father was one."

"Was?"

"He died of a heart attack at 58. Only slightly older than I am."

"Young," Freddie said and blushed again.

"Had he been in the States he would have received a new heart. None was available in Poland then. New hearts are scarce here as well; you have to be put on a waiting list. But I've taken precautions."

"Oh? Do you keep a spare heart on tap?"

"I must. Cardiovascular disease runs in my family. I could expire at any moment."

"You're not serious!" she cried.

"But I am." Gloom filled Szaba's handsome face. "I'm preoccupied by my death. As though it's my mantra."

She felt sorry for Zig as she had for Noah but Szaba was tougher, with greater resources. He could handle his destiny while Greenberg couldn't, she feared.

"The extra heart—is it a pig's?"

"Human. I've just started to grow the arteries in the protein."

"Protein X?" she yelled as the maid left the room.

"Mulheran gave me the substance, yes, produced by your supplier."

"That must have been tempting."

"Yes, and I yielded."

"Under FDA regulations that's illegal."

"The stuff's under lock and key."

She gazed at the ornate surroundings: Muslin valenced draperies, closed at night, the statuette of a nymph on a marble stand (Roman, Romanesque?), the gilt-framed oil paintings of busty nudes with bright pink nipples, wreaths on their heads, enveloped in mist, the dark furniture stuffed with horse hair no doubt, the cabinet filled with reliquaries, the mahogany footstools covered with damask, the Persian rug or was it a carpet?—the ambiance was just too heavy (she couldn't jump over Zig's possessions!), basically European and dust collectors.

"What was your father's occupation?" she inquired.

"Occupation? As in job?" he said mockingly.

"How he spent his time."

"When he wasn't in prison? The American word is hood."

"People who shoot people?"

"If necessary." Szaba's mouth closed to a thin, hard line. "You spent your early years with your dad?"

"The formative ones, yes. In Poland."

"I knew it."

"How?"

"Your speech is a little stilted, as though English isn't quite your natural language."

"Is it my pronunciation?"

"No. How you arrange words in a sentence. The syntax."

"You're observant, darling." He leaned forward and cigar ashes fell on his smoking jacket; he brushed them off. "I arrived in the States when I was 17. The dividing line between those who lose their foreign accents completely is considered to be 16. To master English I had to work extremely hard."

"You always have, I suppose."

"It's a habit. I rarely stop thinking. Now I'm thinking of Imortalon groups…"

"Groups?"

"People proud of their vitality."

She scowled. "Who will organize the groups?"

"Our company. We'll have promotional videos featuring the main attractions, contact sports, mountain climbing and…"

"Well?"

"Sex."

"That's a contact sport?" she questioned.

Zig ignored her sorry attempt at humor. "Imortalon could become a way of life that others might envy."

"Why don't *you* try the drug?" she challenged.

"I'm tempted. Right now I'm more concerned with maximizing profits. I'll form a holding company…." His brow creased as he pondered; he snapped his fingers, "…called Imortalex."

"Clever. I've seen names like that in pharmaceutical ads. We'll need to put it on a letterhead to submit the IND application to the FDA."

"Imortalex will own Imortalon, the manufacturing branch."

"Mirrors. And cigar smoke." She laughed softly.

"We'll need them. Imortalex will issue shares to be traded on the NASDAQ, like other biotech outfits; the stock ought to explode. I'm glad you asked about such matters. You and Mulheran should be rewarded." Zig made rapid calculations on the back of a wine bill. "I'll register 30 million shares priced at a dime. You and Geoff can each purchase 100,000 shares, plus options, for $10,000. A bargain, you'd better believe."

"How can I raise the dough?"

"I'll lend you the money," Zig said instantly.

"No strings?"

"None. Perhaps you'll pay your debt with hard work?"

"On human testing, yes."

"For the SEC to okay the stock, the FDA must approve the drug so the clinical trials *must* succeed," Szaba warned.

"Isn't immortality, or the near approach, be a practical and worthwhile goal?"

"First of all we'll need a statement of purpose," she said.

"Not as good as eradicating cancer but an excellent objective for sure!"

"Well, Imortalon will create history."

"Unless it has nasty side effects."

"It won't," he promised. "The animal studies haven't revealed any."

Szaba's confidence was catching. "No."

He toyed with his silk scarf.

"I'd treasure your advice on redecorating my bedroom."

"Be graceful," she advised.

"Mulheran will be president of Imortalex. You'll be research director."

"Fine," she said.

"Do you think the bed should have a canopy? Come look."

"I have a date with Noah."

"Can't it wait until another day? I have a Cordon Bleu chef."

"Next time, please."

"We'll have to find a spot for Greenberg," Zig muttered. "Some place far away."

Fearful of succumbing, Freddie took the bus to the upper West Side. She thought if Noah is to be banished, what shall I do? Quit the company or accept the inevitable? Such a thin line divides loyalty from being a traitor. All in all, it's best if Greenberg goes. Better for Imortalex, better for me.

She boarded the bus, despising herself.

And why not? She wouldn't feel proud until she adored a man. When would that be? Maybe never.

CHAPTER 9

▼

Freddie had lied to Zig; the date with Noah wasn't until the following night unless she decided to cancel, as she did. Greenberg failed to grab her emotions though he had redeeming characteristics: his love for science, his urge to discover, his skepticism, his faith in God (who on bad days she believed in, sort of) as reflected by his observance of Judaism. He could be selfish but was basically a good man, she prayed.

Zig Szaba, his rival for her affections, carried, like a wand, a sophisticated excitement that bewitched her. He appealed to her younger side—down deep, she was closer to her pom-pom, baton-twirling, cheerleading days than she cared to admit.

If she had to think at all. Maybe the Imortalex stock would soar on invisible wings and she'd be a more-or-less instant millionaire, able to retire to the country, her dream.

What came first? Love, science or money? Wealth had ever appealed to her and love seemed secondary, which left scientific success as her basic goal. Now, though, she had to wonder if the priorities were right. Money had risen in the scheme of things.

To bring herself back to earth, Freddie telephoned Mulheran from her apartment that evening.

"Congratulations, prof."

He recognized her deep voice. "For?"

"Becoming president of Imortalex."

"Oh." Geoff sounded fuddled. "Mr. Szaba offered me the position awhile ago. I accepted after considerable soul-searching."

"As to whether you can accept the responsibilities?"

"Yes. But I'll only be a figurehead."

"You'll have to deal with investment bankers," she cautioned.

"And that gives me the jitters. I'm suffering from a case of nerves."

"A case of vodka is more like it," she started to say but didn't. From his slur, Freddie suspected Mulheran was into a bottle. Are you okay?"

"Certainly," he said.

"Is your vision clear? Do your hands shake?"

"You're presumptuous, Fred-er-ick-a," Geoff said with difficulty. He was irritated.

She had been out of line, although all alcoholics tended to be defensive, as her father was before he traded drinking for gambling, she reflected. Addictions were transferable, it seemed. Maybe Mulheran should move to Atlantic City.

"Szaba stick you for ten grand?"

"I took the money from my retirement account."

Maybe Zig's proposition to Freddie had been a spur-of-the-moment enticement but she assumed he was a man of his word. "Will you receive a salary?"

"Not at first."

"He's a promoter but the investment will pay off," Freddie insisted. "Both of us own a lot of stock plus options that might be worth a fucking ton of money."

"Profanity again."

"It's tedious to bring it up I don't appear to be able to drop the subject but Noah doesn't have a stake in the company."

"Can't he buy stock?"

"He's poor as Jesus. He helps support his synagogue. And Szaba wants to exile him."

"You also wish to?"

"Well....I hate to be disloyal—Noah's a friend, I guess—and he ought to be given a chunk of stock. On the other hand, if he has influence on corporate strategy he might get in the way. We're officers, after all."

"As well as shareholders." A smile lurked in Geoff's telephone whisper.

Freddie had never suspected herself capable of being underhanded. She believed she was above reproach, not given to chicanery. She was pure and innocent, right?

She spoke for Zig, a ventriloquist's dummy, totally under his control.

Mulheran went on, "Yes, Szaba's correct—Greenberg should leave. Sooner or later he'll learn what I'm up to in the lab. Any suggestions?"

"He suspects, I think."

"But he doesn't want to risk antagonizing you?"

"I suppose not." Amazing how little one knew about people you were close to.

"I received a letter from the University of Utah, asking my help. The school has a first-rate genetics department and could use an associate professor. Greenberg, with his Cold Spring Harbor background, is superbly qualified. The pay is excellent. I'll send a letter to Utah tomorrow."

"E-mail them, for God's sake. I'll show you how."

"Who is to inform Greenberg?"

"You, prof. If he's in doubt, I'll try to persuade him."

*   *   *   *

The offer, telephoned by Mulheran and backed up by an e-mail from Utah U (a hard copy would follow) failed to delight Greenberg who, though he stood in awe of the prof, dreaded the unknown. He'd be a member of the faculty but so what? Would that compensate for being away from Freddie?

Not that she was his girlfriend. She'd stubbornly refused to sleep with him and had broken dates as if she didn't respect his feelings. Could she have another man?

Maybe. To Noah, Freddie was awfully hard to read. She kept her emotions to herself. He considered her, well, opaque.

Of course, she might not have gone to bed with the other man yet. The trick must be to tie her down. How?

Perhaps a symbol of his affection and ultimate purpose.

Cold Spring Harbor had a jewelry store.

*   *   *   *

She invited Noah to The Plaza and he arrived from work, wearing scuffed boots, a wrinkled shirt over his windbreaker. "I'm hardly dressed for this."

"Neither am I." She needed a fancier wardrobe no doubt but she was too busy to shop. "The food's a lot better than on the upper West Side, however."

"You've eaten here before, then."

"A while back. With Mr. Szaba."

"The fat cat you referred to."

"He specializes in corporate finance."

"What could you have in common with a *businessman*?"

"He's helping Prof Mulheran with a project," she said.

"Oh," Noah said. To Freddie he seemed doubtful.

"Care for a cocktail?"

"Who's picking up the tab?" he said churlishly.

"I am. Relax. Have fun for a change."

"That's what you told me the last time. You're repeating yourself."

"I must be, I guess."

"I'll have a Scotch and soda, easy on the Scotch," Noah instructed the waiter. "You?"

"A glass of champagne. Veuve Cliquot, please."

"Since when do you order champagne?"

"When I want to toast somebody."

Noah winced. "Who?"

"Wasn't a certain geneticist offered a new job today?" she said coyly.

"You've talked to Mulheran. Well, I told him I'd have to think it over."

"Why?" she said. "Is it the university?"

"Utah U is fine but I'd need a car."

"Buy one."

"I don't wish to leave Cold Spring Harbor."

"You've been there a long while. Time for a change"

"Salt Lake's a Mormon town. Would a Jew be welcome?"

She smiled. "A Jewish polygamist, I guess."

"Don't be cute."

"But what's the real objection?"

He gulped his drink. "Being apart from you."

"The phone. The fax. E-mail."

Noah clenched a fist. "You want me out of the picture because of this Zig guy?"

"No." The other reason was the protein.

"You don't care to watch me deteriorate because of Pompe's," he growled like a wounded animal.

"That would be years from now, if ever. Maybe they'll discover a cure. At Utah U, perhaps."

Noah placed his palms flat on the table, a gesture of surrender. He frowned. "Should I accept?"

"In my opinion? Yes."

"Okay. With a proviso." He straightened up and adjusted his wire-framed glasses. His eyes looked bright behind them. "I'd intended to ask you to marry me tonight. Well, Utah….would you consent to wear an engagement ring?"

The slender ring was encrusted with tiny diamonds. Zig would have given her the moon.

She slipped the ring on the appropriate finger.

He said, "Give me a kiss."

She leaned over and pecked him. "Just one to remember me by. Now let's order. The filet mignon with sauce Béarnaise is exceptional."

*   *   *   *

At home that evening Freddie placed the ring in a drawer. Out of sight, out of mind.

Still, she'd been deceptive. Wasn't that how *they* did business? Come to think of it, accepting the ring *had* been business goddamn it, if only to keep Noah quiet about the protein.

Once she'd compared receiving an engagement ring to getting her college diploma—both required effort and character.

Right? Right.

But what did that say about her character? Something bad perhaps.

CHAPTER 10

▼

The hospital was overcrowded and Freddie needed space to prepare the preliminary data for the FDA-IND application, a short document but requiring hundreds of pages of supporting information with the animal data and a brochure stating the purpose and basic chemistry of the protein molecule.

Szaba offered a room in his vast apartment and the chauffeur hauled the experimental results to the Carlyle where Freddie would collate them and put them on computer. Thousands of animals, in large part rodents, had been and were still being, tested. The study group of rats had almost tripled their normal life spans. She and Zig had figured humans taking Imortalon would live more than two centuries! Was the extrapolation correct or had they made an error? If not, multi-centenarians would dominate the globe.

What would that mean? Demographically, the older population would live in warm places and not a square inch would be left in Florida.

You could buy the product at a pharmacy or, she figured, order the drug electronically by typing i-mortality.com online. That to her was a great idea. Szaba would be thrilled. You'd receive the package next day from UPS.

The drivers might be old as well, staring from the caverns of their eye sockets, from under thatches of white hair. But Imortalon users would be brim full of energy and high spirits.

That was, if nothing went amiss.

Sifting through the numerous cartons, she noticed a notebook that had been thrown into the bottom of a box, as if discarded. Flipping the pages, she saw that a few notations concerned the rhesus monkey, Monk, Freddie had fallen in love with. In Martha's jagged handwriting Freddie read: "Monk has been acting a bit strange. He presses his fists against his head almost like he's in pain. Then he resumes his normal behavior so I guess it's nothing."

Scrawled on the next page: "Chip (a beagle) has tears in her eyes as though she's trying to tell us something. Maybe she's unhappy caged up—I would be for sure! But she's calm for now."

Freddie realized how strange this was—a dog's eyes don't tear. Maybe Martha's imagination had been playing games.

Monk would have been 120 years old or more in human terms had died the previous week, "of natural causes", it seemed. What natural causes? Martha's notes failed to elaborate. Chip, after she'd ceased to eat, had been sacrificed.

Freddie lacked the time to supervise daily operations and left the details to Martha and a small group of medical students. Now she wondered why Monk's and Chip's condition hadn't been brought to her attention. Presumably they hadn't seemed important, though Freddie now realized the creatures might have been in pain.

The trouble with animals was that they couldn't tell you how they felt. Maybe Chip had starved herself deliberately. Dogs were capable of suicide, she believed.

Zig burst into the room. Her expression, she knew, was downcast. "Anything the matter?"

"Have a look at this."

He quickly scrutinized the notebook. "Details," he said impatiently.

"Shouldn't we mention the incidents in the IND application?"

"Other animals show the same pathology?"

"Not that I'm aware of."

"See? Destroy the pages. Why cause ourselves unnecessary problems?"

"But what if...."

"'What if what?"

"Something's wrong with the protein. Suppose it's capable of causing harm?"

"A serious problem would have emerged during the months you've been testing the stuff."

"More than a year with the rodents."

"Isn't that sufficient?"

"Probably. But we should be cautious," she said.

"How cautious?" Zig bristled with impatience. "We're being delayed by trivia…"

"Trivia?" She exploded. "You believe possible side effects aren't significant?"

"But the animals haven't demonstrated any."

"We don't know for sure."

His impatience showed again. "Nonsense!" he yelled.

"Calm down, Zig."

"We must concentrate on the delivery system," Szaba tossed the notebook into a wastebasket.

"Hold on," she said. "You shouldn't destroy data just because you can't explain them. Lots of drugs are on the market despite adverse effects. The PDR..."

"PDR?"

"*The Physicians" Desk Reference* is filled with examples. But essentially we've had no adverse events in the animal trials—almost unheard of—so let's leave the data as is."

"Someone might see the notebook and overreact. They'd think the protein is hazardous in spite of the animal results."

"We should just be careful, that's all."

The corners of Zig's mouth turned down. He looked positively scary and Freddie remembered Carlos. Her body filled with fear.

Szaba must have detected that something perturbed her. He said, "All right. I'll keep the notebook in a safe place. Separated from the other data. Satisfied?"

"Yes," she mumbled.

"So," he said, rapidly changing the subject, "how shall people take Imortalon? Injections?"

Freddie tried to concentrate on pharmacology.

"That might require visits to the doctor which would make the drug prohibitively expensive. As things are, most folks won't be able to afford it. Besides, I doubt if muscle would absorb the protein."

"In a drink?" Zig quizzed.

"As if for heartburn, so-called. Forget it. Heartburn's not serious. Aging is," she declared.

"A pill? A tablet?"

"Proteins can't be administered in tablets. They'd be destroyed by the digestive process. To do any good, the drug would have to reach the intestines. Maybe a capsule to enclose a powder? A time-release capsule designed to dissolve in the small intestine?"

"A capsule?" Zig smoothed his wavy gray hair and smiled handsomely. "Yes, a capsule might do the trick. We'll require experts."

Where would he find them? Szaba had connections in the biotech field. He'd spent most of his life trying to make money there.

"Aren't you afraid someone will steal the Imortalon concept?"

He laughed easily. No, he wasn't. Mulheran owned the patents to the wonder drug. And Szaba knew experts from a Boston outfit he felt he could trust.

∗   ∗   ∗   ∗

The experts arrived as the Carlyle during the next few days, well-dressed men in business suits. Freddie compiled notes on the pilot plant which would be needed to manufacture the protein in capsule from:

> *A large, cylindrical, stainless steel, electrically-heated tank to grow the monkey virus; the contents of the tank will arrange themselves by molecular weight, aided by air pressure…*

"The virus", her notes went on, "will be on the top layer; a sterile suction device with filters will remove the virus first and it will be kept, frozen, for future use. I repeat: *the virus causes a mild cold in simians but has no known effect on humans.*"

That's what Mulheran had claimed and she had no reason to doubt him. A leading authority, he must have checked the scientific literature. Geoff was thorough, above all. Of course, he sometimes seemed a bit distracted, perhaps by dreams of wealth, fueled by alcohol.

"The pure protein will constitute the bottom layer. It will be suctioned into a vacuum tube with perforations and slowly flow into a centrifuge that forces the liquid (which has become a powder in the centrifuge) into softgel capsules through needles while the protein remains warm. The capsules are composed of vegetable gelatin. The microscopic hole in the banded capsule is instantly resealed and the capsules enter a chute in which they are automatically counted and dropped into plastic jars. The jars are given a lot number and placed in cartons by hand for shipment to pharmacies, which may sell them only on prescription.

"We will require a staff: a Human Resources consultant to put together the company; lawyers to extend patent protection globally; a Regulatory Affairs Director to deal with the FDA post-marketing regulations; a pharmavigilence team to address product concerns; a Data Manager to head up the clinical trials; numerous technicians and service people…

"A small factory, which the FDA must approve, with adequate room for security guards, loading platforms, forklifts, access to transportation, etc. And we must keep in mind space for expansion if the product takes off," she typed.

Szaba said, "A major accomplishment. Nothing like Imortalon has ever existed, not even close. People can actually purchase extra years."

"I've figured out an easy way to do that. You need only type on the computer, "i-mortality dot com."

"Brilliant." He smiled.

"But I forgot. Doctors would have to write a prescription."

"We'll find amenable doctors. He massaged her neck and Freddie, calmer now, continued typing.

She glanced up. "What's your view on how they'd use the extra years they buy?"

"Nothing unusual. They'll enjoy a slice of pizza, a round of golf, a bridge game, the shopping center, movies, and an occasional orgasm to anticipate."

"You're too practical, Zig," she said mildly shocked. "They could improve their minds. Attend art galleries and lectures. Retirement could become much more fulfilling."

"If you ask me, they'll finally get round to planting the garden, raking the lawn, cleaning out the attic, having a tag sale, knowing the end of their favorite soap opera. All that's plenty for most."

"Not I," she murmured. "When I'm old I'll still want romance."

He stroked her head. "You're a confirmed idealist, Freddie."

"You have twice my years, Zig. You must be far wiser."

"I'd be even wiser if I lived longer."

"Where's the proof of that? Old people aren't especially known for wisdom. They're more likely to forget."

"But not me."

What makes you think so?"

"I give myself, even now, constant memory checks. Do I recall the names of people I've only briefly met? Do I remember the color of their eyes?"

"Close yours. Describe mine."

"Green with brown flecks."

"And my hair?"

"Don't be silly. Blond, of course."

"My chin?"

"Pointed like a witch's."

She frowned. "My upper lip?"

"Short. Stubborn. And very kissable."

"Watch it! I can bite."

"I'm not afraid." Zig smiled with masculine confidence.

"But I am. Open your eyes. Tell me what you've learned so far."

"Hard to summarize."

"Try," she urged.

"My goals? Among them, to stay as I am until I'm ready to die."

"Impossible! Not even Imortalon can give you that. Extend one's life but…."

"No? Some day, perhaps, I'll show you."

"Okay." She hesitated. "Your other goals?"

"To have eternal wealth."

"Like the Egyptian pharaohs? They don't have banks in the pyramids. You wouldn't be around to spend the pounds or whatever the goddam Egyptian currency is."

"I wouldn't bet on that," Szaba said as though he half expected to live forever. "I shall though."

Zig shrugged his broad shoulders. "In the meanwhile, my main objective is you, Freddie," he said in a low, urgent voice and bent to kiss her.

She turned her face away. "I'd prefer to concentrate on ARP at the moment."

"ARP? Animal Rescue…?"

"Aging Retardant Protein."

"Come again? Something that retards us?"

"Something that slows the aging process. And I wish *you'd* slow down." Lay off, she meant.

CHAPTER 11

▼

Standing, Freddie became acutely conscious of Szaba's black eyes examining her beautiful hips. At least he'd said they were beautiful. To her they were just plain hips, narrowing and sloping up to her thin waistline and, at that moment, encircled by tight-fitting denim pants enclosing her groin and her skinny legs. Szaba had called her sexy but she preferred to be thought of as sensuous and she was, she supposed.

She licked her lips and told Zig she'd talked with an FDA safety officer who requested information on how the protein would be manufactured. Rather than reveal the product's appellation, she'd invented another and ARP was the acronym.

"I worried 'Imortalon' might reveal what it actually is, if word gets around. You know: a great name for a miracle drug."

He kind of hiccupped from excitement. "Clever. But it should really be ARP-1."

"One?"

"The '1' designates the first of a product line."

"So we'd have additional products?"

He said he'd been considering a remedy for Alzheimer's, based on the magic protein. "I'm afraid the drug might be viewed as simply cosmetic by the FDA."

"I've already thought of that," she said. "Why can't aging be treated as a disease?"

"Pardon? A *disease?*"

"A disease that could be put into remission for any number of years."

"Like cancer?" he asked.

"Well, perhaps," she said.

"At least we can claim that it does. Imortalon will get rid of the symptoms of aging, mainly physical weakness, we'll say."

"Yes. The drug will make you strong."

"Not like steroids, though," she said.

"Steroids drive people crazy. Imortalon won't," Zig declared.

"At least I hope not." She looked at Zig. "Anyway, the drug *will* be anti-aging."

Zig blinked. "Inspired! Absolutely inspired! That notion too must remain secret."

Oh God, she thought, so much is secret. The government is secretive, business is secretive, Szaba is secretive, I'm secretive—where will it fucking end? "From whom?" she asked.

"Competitors. Our product will spawn them by the dozens. You'll have herbal cures, exotic teas, exclusive patented potions, diet supplements, all promising relief from aging. Since they're neither a food nor a drug, the FDA can't regulate them."

"But would they be effective?"

"Without the protein? About as good as aphrodisiacs made of elephant tusks. The Asians pay high prices for them. They've convinced themselves of their utility."

"Wish-fulfillment? Like people wishing they were young? Time is important to our perceptions, isn't it?" said she.

"Exactly. If you've ceased aging, there *is* no time. Literally. A freeze frame. When you begin aging again the bioclock starts to tick once more."

"So for a brief period you're immortal," she said.

"Stem cells can be immortalized which doesn't seem to violate the laws of nature."

"Except for the Hayflick Limit."

"Pardon?"

"In the early sixties, Dr. Leonard Hayflick, a cell biologist, discovered decades ago that tissue cells grown in Petrie dishes divide about fifty times but become shorter until they reach a critical minimum length and enter a mortal crisis. The telomerse gene seems to make them normal again but it's still in development."

"The protein solves the Hayflick problem?" he inquired.

"So it appears."

Szaba seemed to muse darkly. "Tissue cells will no longer be able to die abruptly."

"Nor will Imortalon users."

"Of course! Instead of aging they'd be filled with verve."

"Verve? As in champagne?"

"Excitement. Gaiety. At having so much quality time in front of one," Szaba positively bubbled.

"Before you get carried away, I should remind you we will need a place to manufacture the drug."

"I'll scout locations. New Jersey's a logical place. Merck is there. So's Pfizer."

"Surely we can't compete with the pharmaceutical giants," she said.

"But we can. We possess the multi-billion dollar molecule, not they."

Freddie thought about millions, even billions, of dollars especially in the context of *we*. But she was more interested in science than she'd ever be in profits, right?

"How do we get our name out there?" she asked.

"We'll need publicity."

Freddie opposed publicity as a matter of principle. To her it contradicted the very idea of science which depended on experiments, probably in a lab; independently verified. She was even against advertising because it confused consumers. Freddie had always been obstinate and nothing would change that.

Frederick was a purist too, in his own way; perhaps she'd inherited the trait. But she didn't regard herself as inflexible.

*   *   *   *

Pharmaceutical outfits often hire publicity personnel well in advance of FDA product approval; Szaba put on the payroll a public relations person for Imortalex, Inc., the parent company. Her name was Iris Dove and she'd worked for a glossy magazine that publicized ethical drugs.

Freddie first encountered the p.r. lady in Zig's den. Short, slim, vivacious, with a rather regal English accent, she said to Szaba as he pored through promotional pamphlets New Jersey had sent him, "Might the maid sweep up your cigar ashes?"

Maid? Freddie thought. She'd been cleaning the office Zig had provided in his labyrinthine apartment and was wearing an apron. By contrast, Iris had on spike heels, cashmere skirt, and silk blouse cut so low it almost revealed the nipples. Maybe Szaba had purchased the clothes.

He said, "Freddie's a corporate officer. Say hello, Iris."

Iris' fingernails were crimson, her eyes brown and her brown hair a mass of curls, as Carlos' had been. She seemed to be slightly older than Freddie, 35 perhaps.

"You've just been to the beauty shop," Freddie commented.

"Yep. How do I look?"

"Terrific. What beauty shop?"

"On Madison Avenue."

"And where did you buy the rags?"

"Mad Av," Iris said.

"A boutique, huh?"

"Yeah," Iris said, minus the English accent.

Freddie laughed. "I think we'll be friends. Where are you from?"

"Hoboken, New Jersey."

"My native state."

"Swell!"

"What did you do before the magazine?" Freddie asked suspiciously.

"I went to an all-girl college."

"Ever been married?"

"Briefly. I had it annulled."

"Why?"

"My former husband couldn't perform. He's a…"

"Homosexual?"

"Better believe it. Have you been married?"

"No."

"Good! We're sisters under the skin. I'm sure we can work together." Iris gazed at Freddie who returned the stare.

"I warn you—I'm against the tricks of your trade."

"Why?"

"They're nothing more than legalized fraud."

"But necessary for success."

"We'll see."

Iris winked. "We need an image."

"Of?"

"A company full of ooomph, that pours out ideas like a fountain."

Zig stepped into earshot. He said, "A fountain of youth," Zig said.

"Like yourself, Mr. Szaba."

"I try."

"To keep it up?" Iris seemed to taunt.

Zig's smile concealed anger, Freddie knew. The p.r. lady's humor, well-intentioned, meant to be casual joking, went too far and Szaba reacted. But he smoothly regained his composure as Iris went on, "A pharmaceutical outfit that never tires in the quest for...."

"What?" Freddie said.

"Oh, excellence, flawlessness, preeminence, superiority, accomplishments, in a word, perfection, a paradigm."

"Like me," Zig said and Freddie wondered why he bothered to puff himself up. Was he insecure? Were most men insecure?

Yes, and their antidote was women. Women who flattered them, made them feel, if not heroic, then attractive and successful.

Exactly," Iris said. "At any rate we must present the company in the best possible light. Our investors must have faith in management."

"They shall," Szaba pledged.

"I'll convey the message to the media," Iris said and grinned at Freddie.

"The message is?" Freddie asked. She looked at the p.r. lady. Iris said, "The company that's destined to be immortal. Something like that should be our slogan."

"Trademarked," Szaba said. "All the major pharmaceutical houses are extremely boastful. We must be too. If we don't praise ourselves, who shall for God's sake?"

"You're wise, Mr. Zig," Iris said. "Modest companies—the ones that don't make extravagant claims, who fail to continually pat themselves on the back, singing their own praises—fall by the wayside."

"Women as well," Szaba said. "Especially if they intend to rise in business."

Freddie had decided she wanted, fervently, to succeed. Perhaps p.r. wasn't such a bad idea, after all. Or Iris.

*   *   *   *

Szaba gaped when he saw Freddie decked out in Mad Av splendor. "You could be a fashion model."

"That's what Noah said."

"Greenberg? Listen to me, not him."

"Okay, Zig," she said submissively.

"You'll follow my orders?"

"Depends on how demanding you are."

"Very, perhaps."

"Oh."

"Will Greenberg stay in Salt Lake City?"

"If I wish him to, I think. He's not happy there but he's reasonably content. For Noah, that is. He always complains."

"But not about expenses, I trust," said Szaba who, she knew, had secretly underwritten the costs of relocating Greenberg.

"No. But I'll need financial help with the finery."

"Money's no problem once we have FDA approval."

*   *   *   *

Pleased by her appearance and the use of Zig's credit card, Freddie returned to the boutique for a few more rags. Glancing in the full-length mirror, like a clothes horse, she explored various poses: she frowned, smiled, wiggled her hips, bared her teeth, leered lasciviously, thrust her pelvis forward, and shook her head covered now with blond ringlets, as if in silent rebuke for childish behavior. She was radiant and prayed she wouldn't soon lose her luster.

The rash hadn't returned in months, ever since….she tried to remember.

She felt she could put her mark on men. The time to strike was when the curler was hot.

*   *   *   *

Needing a friend in high places, Freddie phoned the FDA safety officer whose name had been stamped on the IND submission and with whom she'd discussed manufacturing ARP. Now she claimed she was having trouble with the protocol and needed assistance. He obligingly suggested she visit Washington and she boarded Amtrak at Penn Station.

*   *   *   *

As the train rolled across the drainage ditches, separated by land, euphemistically called meadows, she looked through the window reflectively. The steady pounding of the wheels brought back the days she'd traveled to New York City with her dad to catch a Broadway show, her mother being so often sick. They hadn't known at that point she was fatally ill with cancer. That was the reason Freddie had relied so heavily on her father and he'd rarely let her down.

Could she expect the same from Szaba? Like her father, at least in recent years, Zig was a compulsive gambler, only he didn't seek action at the poker table. He was staking his chips on Imortalon—the wonder drug had to be just that, a wonder. But, if Imortalon succeeded could she rely on him? Would he contribute to science? Somehow she doubted him. Why?

Perhaps, although from Europe he lacked her father's strong suit, tradition, not Noah's Jewish tradition but *American* tradition, that Frederick was steeped in. He traced his roots to Colonial days in Virginia; he wasn't a recent immigrant like the Pole Zig, who was slippery, deeply slippery and manipulative.

Her mind raced back to Carlos. Poor Carlos, the Latino on the sidewalk, a knife in his back. Could something similar lie in wait for her?

The train stopped briefly at Newark and she eyed the slums around the depot. She enjoyed inventing jokes and one occurred to her now. What would you have if you developed a fatal illness at a railroad station? A terminal illness!

She smiled, then grimaced. Death always occupied her thoughts, as did Szaba.

*   *   *   *

Theodore Stover appeared to be in his early 40's, easygoing, relaxed, with a thick brown beard, moist around the mouth like a gap in a rain forest. The clearing opened as he inspected Freddie's business card and surveyed her across his desk.

"You don't fit the picture."

"Picture?"

"The corporate image. You're alone. Where's your team? I usually get a bunch of highly-paid consultants. You're young and…"

"Go on. Say it. Inexperienced."

"I was going to say attractive."

He'd love to hit on me. She uncrossed her ankles so as not to seem too tightly wound.

"The picture's one thing; reality's another. The fact is, I'm an…." She withdrew "asshole", such phrasing might be inappropriate in a sanitized governmental setting…"a dummy and I need help with the protocol for human testing."

"That's hardly the normal procedure. We don't bend over backwards to…well, I'll give you assistance if I can."

The rain forest offered a branch to the desolate bird, lost in the bureaucratic surroundings. Freddie removed the completed IND from her shoulder bag and Stover perused it. "What's this ARP supposed to accomplish?"

"I believe we made that clear. To keep people younger."

"*Looking* younger? They could have face lifts, body tucks, liposuction…."

She objected: "Plus with the protein, more vigorous sex lives."

"New drugs, which improve circulation and increase hormonal activity, are being introduced for that purpose. Although old age doesn't mean what it did before geriatrics. Ten years ago, the medical profession recognized the need to develop a specialty for this demographic group. Diseases we associate with age— Alzheimer's, Parkinson's, osteoporosis, osteoarthritis, stroke, hypertension, anxiety, high cholesterol, incontinence, diabetes—there's no end to them and they can be controlled with the potent new drugs. You can get a list of them on the internet, Aging dot com."

She attempted a smile. "Okay. To postpone aging almost indefinitely."

Nothing seemed to surprise Stover. "You're playing with words. Older…a few more facial lines. The bell tolls…"

"Listen," said she, exasperated, "those on an ARP regimen have far fewer medical problems. They won't need doctors, hospitals, expensive drugs or HMOs for years. The Baby Boomers…."

"Seventy-seven million of them," he said.

"…will be our main market," she predicted.

"…are the least informed generation in American history. Except for their kids, Generation X."

"How did you reach that conclusion?" she asked breathlessly, hoping her flirting wasn't too obvious.

"From the medical commercials on TV. Those folks accept the wildest claims with nary a murmur of protest. You'd think half the people are constipated. Or the root that's supposed to improve memory. Hah! Were folks tested for memory enhancement? You wouldn't resort to trickery, would you?"

"No." She smiled and narrowed her green eyes. "But the FDA must approve our application."

The rain forest grinned. "May I invite you to dinner?"

A bear in the clearing. "Sorry, I have to get back to work. You'll give me tips?"

"Uh-huh. I'll prepare the traditional formal responses in a few days instead of the usual thirty."

"And might we have dinner when I'm next in Washington?"

"I'll give you my home address and phone number. You'll be in touch?"

"I promise."

*   *   *   *

Szaba concurred with Freddie's appraisal: Stover might be valuable in winning speedy FDA approval for human testing. And he had no doubt Imortalon would ultimately be allowed to reach the market.

As Freddie had suggested Zig began to scout the area adjacent to the Newark train depot for a factory building. They'd need to produce the protein in large enough amounts for human subjects. It would be the pilot project. Szaba reported, "The neighborhood is rundown with insufficient lighting. The streets are dangerous."

"So why locate there?" she asked.

"Because it's cheap."

"Anything specific in mind?"

"An abandoned warehouse. It mustn't cost more than we've allocated in the budget projection, but, just the same, we need enough class to be featured in *Pharmaceutical Executive* magazine—you understand, our expectations, our future image. I'd give the warehouse a facelift, redo the old brick with a façade which allows you to do Greek columns inexpensively and with the right colors, we'll have the image we want. So it's a poor location! The photographers will ignore the surroundings and concentrate on the refurbished building. I have the keys. I'll show you if you'd like."

"I'd like." She now felt comfortable with Szaba but for how long, she had to ask.

Perhaps almost forever. She calculated the difference in their ages: about 30 years (he'd never quite told her his exact age). He remained sharp and vigorous, kept his perspective, refused to succumb to grandiose visions.

And she? She'd have to accommodate him until he crossed the line. Then she'd stand up and fight like a man.

Trouble was, could she be sure when he'd crossed the line? Being devious seemed to explain his essence. Or did it?

CHAPTER 12

▼

The silver Daimler passed through the Holland Tunnel. The river surrounding them reminded Freddie of water and so, as a practical person, she asked, "When we manufacture the protein, couldn't we contaminate the water supply? Have we notified the Environmental Protection Agency?"

"We'll meet the requirements," Zig said blandly.

"How about the Occupational Safety folks, OSHA?"

"Them too."

"And if we don't?"

"The proper people will be taken care of." He fingered his palm.

The Daimler entered a narrow street. Except for the roar of a train and car horns from a nearby avenue, the street was silent and deserted, although a bodega occupied one corner and clothing draped from windows, indicating rooming houses. Garbage littered the pavements.

"Somebody actually lives here," she marveled.

"So it seems."

A Mustang was parked before a large, shuttered building that had to be the warehouse. "Who does the car belong to?"

"Len Veere, our security chief. He's inside."

"I've never met him, have I?"

Szaba failed to respond.

When she saw the dark, heavy-set man, she instantly realized she'd encountered him in the hospital corridor the day before Carlos had been stabbed. Mere coincidence?

Veere looked at her bleakly. With a grease pencil he sketched oblong boxes on the wall.

"What are they supposed to be? Coffins?"

"No, miss. Rifle racks."

"We'll have them built once we own the place," Zig said. "It'll be twelve thousand square feet which ought to be enough to start with."

"The place will be a fortress," Veere stated.

"Why?" Freddie asked.

Veere glanced at Szaba who took gloves from his sportscoat and put them on. "Filthy in here."

"Don't worry, boss. A crew will clean it up," Veere said.

Zig said, "This is a rough neighborhood and we'll have equipment to protect. How many electrical outlets will you need, Len?"

"For the closed-circuit TV monitors, the infrared scanners and the computers to help identify strangers at the door? Well…plus the DC stun gun if the visitors prove hostile…"

"Make sure you don't stun my European pals," Szaba said lightly.

"How would Veere know they're foreign?" Freddie asked.

"By their typical Polish three-piece suits and Polish accents. Plus the fact they'd return the fire and shoot to kill. Come, Freddie, see the rest." He gestured toward a stairway.

She went first, conscious of his black eyes on her rear. No, she wouldn't move her hips sexily—save that sort of thing for the mirror. Here she was in an abandoned warehouse which hardly seemed the right place to play games, though she had the damnedest urge to flirt. When didn't she!

She wouldn't show it. She preferred to be opaque, hidden. Let the men be transparent, their desires as clear as if witnessed through a pane of glass.

She ascended the stairs, her short skirt exposing slender calves.

He passed her on the landing and pointed to chalk marks on the floor. "This is where the heated tanks will be and over here the freezer to store the monkey virus. We'll need a generator to maintain the-40°C in case of power failure."

"The freezer must be locked," she said. "We don't know much about the virus. It's not dangerous but we're forced to take precautions as though the stuff might be hazardous to humans, though that's a long shot and there's no empirical proof."

"And the FDA hasn't objected so far," Zig said thoughtfully. "They're satisfied with our procedures."

"Nonetheless, if there's the slightest sign of trouble, the virus must be destroyed," Freddie warned.

"How?"

"A fumigant, maybe."

"Unless the virus is immortal."

"Not a chance in hell," she declared.

Szaba said abruptly, "I've all but decided to buy the warehouse. I'm sure the owner will accept my terms. We're finally off the ground."

"Now comes the hard part, human testing."

"Which will be a breeze," Zig said and stared at her eagerly, as though she would be a breeze too.

*   *   *   *

On the way back to Manhattan, Zig closed the panel separating them from the driver and kissed her. At first Freddie refused to respond but under his warmth and pressure, she gradually opened her lips and felt the tip of his tongue exploring her mouth, tentatively at first then with genuine ardor.

Freddie remembered the joke about the space captain who seduced the female ruler of a distant planet, who said to him, "But that's how we make cars."

What *were* such jokes? Protective mechanisms against fear? But, for her, sex constituted a serious act, nothing to laugh about.

*   *   *   *

She verged on accepting Zig as her lover but he had to pass the human test and maybe he'd fail. She needed someone to emulate, to set one's standards by, and, when she got right down to it, the one individual on earth she truly admired was her father.

At the very least her lover had to be considerate, unlike Noah who was self-centered but remained on Freddie's mind.

From her apartment later on she phoned Greenberg again in Salt Lake City. "How's it going?"

"Fine, I guess, but I wish you were here."

She thought of Szaba. "I'd love to be." She was getting accustomed to fibs.

"Any news?" he asked.

Of the protein, he meant of course, and she had to distract him, a task made easier because such experiments were typically drawn-out and required virtually unlimited time. He'd assume she hadn't definitive results as to the molecule's possible use as yet or else he would have been informed.

And if he meant Freddie's life, he certainly didn't want to know too much—answers might have unsettled him.

She said quickly, "You're aware I've been keeping old horses in New Jersey? Well, I bought another and it died."

"Oh." The subject of animals bored Noah.

What was the cause of death? she again wondered. Her father had been feeding the nags oats with the magic protein, she had no idea how much. An old mare had been unexpectedly frisky and then it had tried to kick her dad according to him, and then had died without any prior symptoms.

The protein hadn't conferred extra years on the mare—perhaps it didn't work on animals that large.

"Are you there?" Noah asked.

"I was thinking."

"Of the lab?"

"No."

"Of our nuptials then?" She couldn't disguise the hardness in her voice.

"Have I choice?" He laughed resentfully. "I love you, Freddie."

"Me too."

Like most men, Noah didn't listen carefully. If he had he'd have heard "me too" meant herself, an egotist. Who did she remind herself of? She knew in a flash. Szaba!

Noah hadn't finished. "If you need help, don't hesitate to call. But I'm afraid you're lying."

What made him think she wasn't?

CHAPTER 13

▼

Freddie then went to Short Hills to visit her father and inspect the horses.

The surviving equines appeared to be in fine fettle but not her dad. He wasn't old, in his sixties, but his spirit had taken a beating when his wife died and he hadn't fully recovered.

As he wasn't ashamed to admit Frederick's wealth had been inherited. The Fergusons, hard-working Irishmen, had gone into timber and sawmills. Frederick, an only child, as was his daughter, had attended Princeton University and attempted to run the family business after his father had been killed in a car crash. Frederick displayed a lassitude toward wood products, preferring to concentrate on his hobbies and writing light verse. He'd let the business go to seed. He loved attending Broadway musicals and Freddie remembered her parents in what they referred rather quaintly as evening clothes.

When her mother died of ovarian cancer, Frederick had gone berserk. He'd sold the business and turned into a gambler, finding solace at the low-stakes Atlantic City poker tables. He lost but by then he didn't have much to lose. He'd kept the tiny farm near Short Hills and, when there, become a virtual recluse.

Freddie's reaction to her mother's passage and her dad's quirky behavior had been to forget luxury and throw herself into science. She'd intended to be plain and studious, at least until Zygmunt Szaba had come along.

In sharp contrast to the French food she'd been eating with Zig at fancy restaurants, Freddie's father served pork-and-beans from a can. "Dad," she said, fork hovering. "Did you provoke the mare before she tried to kick you?"

"She was old and cantankerous, that's all," Frederick said sniffily. His thick gray hair belied his age; he wore glasses not because his vision was poor but to see the cards around the poker table.

"Yes but were you standing close behind her?"

"I'm...not certain."

"Maybe I'd had a couple." He angled his head at the whiskey bottle on the counter.

Jesus, she thought, another Mulheran. No. Frederick drank but wasn't an alcoholic. When the stakes were high, he stopped.

"And maybe you hadn't. Did you have a drink this afternoon?"

"Several. Before you came. I was excited by your dropping in."

"The drinks. Morning, right?"

"I guess," he said vaguely.

"Frederick, this is important. Did you provoke the mare?"

"I don't think so."

"Dad, remember the Cole Porter lyric you used to sing?"

"What was the show?"

"'Let's Do It', I believe."

"The song is the same as the show's title. My favorite." He recited: "'Penguins in flocks, on the rocks do it, Even little cuckoos in their clocks do it, Let's do it, Let's fall in love'....Want more? 'In shallow shoals English soles do it....'"

Freddie groaned. Her father's memory was splendid, which meant the mare had no reason to attack him. Unless the protein had caused the old mare to turn hostile before it died.

The results were inconclusive at best.

So were their arguments over gambling. "What's your favorite card game, dad?" she asked.

"Five card draw."

"That's poker?"

"Of course."

"Deuces wild?"

"No wild cards permitted."

"Why?"

"Screws up the odds in favor of blind luck."

"Poker isn't blind luck?"

"It's more akin to mathematics."

Freddie gave a frustrated sigh. "I don't remember you as being good with figures."

"I had to learn of necessity."

"Sounds boring."

"Boredom is often the price of success, daughter."

"But you don't usually win, dad. Why not quit?"

"Never!"

Nor would she. They were quintessentially stubborn, Freddie reminded herself.

*   *   *   *

Thirty days had passed since the filing of the IND without major objections from the FDA. The bureaucratic silence meant human testing could begin.

Freddie said to Szaba, "As Mr. Stover remarked in his comments on the protocol, we'll need not the twelve we planned on but twenty healthy volunteers. All can be recruited locally—it doesn't matter. They'll be given the capsules of the protein by a clinical physician, someone from the hospital, I guess. They'll have to visit five or six times to check their blood, muscles, etc., for toxicity and side effects. The volunteers will be paid modestly, as will the physician."

"Is that all?" said Zig wearily.

"No. We'll need an IRB—an Independent Review Board, also physicians. They'll evaluate the ethics of our Phase I testing."

"Phase One? My God, are there others?"

"Yes, II and III. And post-marketing, Phase IV," she insisted.

"You're the research director. You organize the procedure. Then let's take a brief vacation."

"To?"

"The Berkshire Mountains. I own, well, a castle there."

"But no hanky-panky, okay?"

"Understood," Zig said winningly. "I'll tell Mark, my chauffeur."

Castle. Hanky-panky. Room for misinterpretation, thought Freddie.

Would she surrender?

CHAPTER 14

▼

A few days afterward they motored to Massachusetts. It was a gorgeous day and the trees were changing to fall colors. More than a year had passed since the experiment with Greenberg's protein had started. Freddie felt proud of herself because of Imortalon.

Just outside Great Barrington the limo climbed a steep hill with a structure on top. Like a rich man's fantasy. Maybe Szaba's expectation of having unlimited wealth was also a fantasy, she thought.

As Mark, who was shaped like a horseshoe, with round shoulders and long, spindly arms—she'd never actually seen his fact, protected by his cap and visor, and long white hair—carried their bags inside, Zig showed off the magnificent views.

The house—all right a mini, art deco castle—was also spectacular; the tapestries, the medieval suits of armor the wide wooden staircase leading to the upper floor, the leather-bound books in the library, the old portraits in the spacious dining room.

"Are those your ancestors?"

"God no! I almost wish they were. The furnishings are leased. They're meant to impress the summer people who pay a big enough rent to sustain the house year round."

"You can't afford to?"

"No." He added, with a wry expression. "Besides I don't have many ancestors."

"Why?" she queried.

His shoulders slumped. "Because of an inherited illness."

"Not Pompe's disease?"

Szaba stared at her. "Congenital heart failure."

"How could *both* men in her life have defective genes? A twist of fate. Life was ironic.

"And you're susceptible?"

"Who knows?" Zig said bitterly. "The disease is supposed to strike every other generation, suddenly and without warning...."

"Doctors can't detect it?"

He shook his dark head. "The onset can't be predicted. One dies just like *that*."

"But surely you keep track of the generations," she said.

"No way. With so much intrabreeding in my family—central Europe has been in turmoil for centuries—it's hard to tell what a generation is. I have half-sisters and half-brothers."

"Where were you born, Zig?"

"In Poland, right after the end of the Second World War. I grew up under the Communists. My father dispatched me to America to escape the struggles and supported me the best he could. I attended a polytech school—I'd planned to become a biological engineer—but I surrendered to my basic instincts and majored in business at NYU. I apprenticed with a Wall Street firm which even then had an interest in biotechnology, but soon struck out on my own. One of my earliest clients was Professor Mulheran."

"So that's the connection!"

"But Geoff got—what's the word?—beaten to the punch," Szaba said in a resigned voice. "Stolen from would be more accurate. Perhaps it was for the best because the FDA failed to approve the anti-cholesterol product. Still, the venture made certain people question my judgment."

"You have fatalistic streak, Zig," she said sympathetically.

"I forbid you to pity me. I have a plan. I'll show you if you'll pledge to keep it confidential."

"I will," Freddie breathed.

Szaba patted his jacket and called, "Mark? He has the keys."

The chauffeur arrived instantly. His face—she saw his visage for the first time—was nearly round, with a low brow, bulging cheeks, ears that seemed glued to his head. He had flared nostrils you could almost put your fingers in, as if he were a bowling ball. Freddie thought of the retainers who'd served Count Dracula and Dr. Frankenstein, at least in the movies, and tried not to smile.

Szaba stared at her and whispered, "Mark suffers from the PKU syndrome..."

"What's that?"

"It's extremely rare, occurring in about one of ten thousand births. Phenylke-tonuria comes from an overabundance of the amino acid phenylalanine in body tissues and leads to brain starvation. The condition used to account for one percent of mental defectives but, with blood tests and special diets, PKU retardation is increasingly rare. A few, though, slip through the safety nets. Mark was among them. His IQ is extremely low."

"Nice of you to give him a job. Is he safe to be chauffeured by?"

"The best. He keeps his eyes totally on the road. Besides who else would hire him? He follows my instructions slavishly, driving from Manhattan in all sorts of weather to take care of….oh, never mind. You'll find out soon enough. I hope you have a strong stomach."

"I work in a lab, let me remind you."

"The door, Mark," Zig bellowed.

They followed the chauffeur down marble steps overlaid by a velvet rug. Mark tried the pockets of his buff uniform, sighed, screwed up his face and finally removed from around his neck a large copper loop from which keys dangled. He turned two locks in a brass-studded door which swung open on well-oiled hinges.

"Mark attends to details," Zig commented.

"He changes light bulbs? It's dark in there."

"No. The lighting's hi-tech fluorescent with ecotron balance. The mercury in the tubes gives off wavelengths in the infrared range and impairs eyesight."

He took goggles from a hook on the wall and gave her a pair. They put them on.

The scene was surreal: a large glass receptacle—oxygenated she suspected from the bubbles in the thick liquid—filled with, oh God.

She peered, not being immediately able to determine what the giant jar contained although the shapes seemed familiar. Twisted and convoluted, they reminded her of modern art. Dali or Balthus, perhaps.

Bacon. Meat.

"Spare parts," Zig said. "That they've survived represents a stunning victory over death."

Freddie recognized a small intestine.

"Is it human?" she cried.

"Not meant for tractors," Zig said mockingly

"Oh," she murmured, inspecting the jar more closely. "Muscles. I can't find them."

"Artificial muscles are under development with a sort of silk composed of Orlon. The synthetic muscles will be stronger than normal ones."

"Suppose the body rejects the new parts?"

"It won't if I add a snippet of my DNA to the protein broth."

"A brain? I don't see one."

"I'd use my own. Why have something inferior?"

"What if you had a stroke or brain tumor?"

"I'd probably decide to die."

Freddie admired Zig's scientific skills but was shocked by his obsession with longevity.

He went on, "I regard myself as a guinea pig. If I succeed, I'll have paved the way for others. If I fail, well…"

"Isn't that a bit suicidal?"

"I've always considered that option."

"But if you lived you could be a virtual cyborg. But not even a cyborg can exist forever."

"Probably," Szaba seemed to agree. "Only wealth is eternal."

"Have you heirs, Zig?"

"Negative. My parents are deceased and nobody is left in Poland I care about. Maybe you'll be my heir, Freddie."

"I believe you're trying to bribe me, Zig." She thought of the mare. "Side effects are not entirely out of the question, you know."

"They would have surfaced by now."

"We need the human testing to be utterly sure. Even then…."

"I'm healthy. Why worry yourself?" Zig said.

"I do though. And why are you taking the drug?"

"A whim!"

"Be serious," Freddie insisted.

"All right. So I won't grow old before you do."

"You must be kidding!"

Her amusement was infectious and Zig grinned. "I'll remain the same until you catch up with me. By then, you'll be using Imortalon too."

"Would I?" She puckered her lips, attractively she hoped.

"Everyone will. Finally, I'll become decrepit and require the body parts."

She frowned. "You're insane, Szaba."

"Oh, I doubt that, I very much doubt that."

"You're suggesting a kind of aging leapfrog."

"In a sense. When I'm too feeble and you're still youngish you'd find another guy. I wouldn't be...."

"Jealous?" she asked.

He hesitated. "More port?"

"No. I need a clear head when I'm dealing with you. You really wouldn't be jealous?"

"Well..."

"Listen Zig, you want us to be permanent? Is that the idea?"

"Until eternity," Zig said "whenever that is."

"Tomorrow, maybe," Freddie said and suddenly felt like crying. Eternity to her equaled death.

He must have intuited her mood and, with surprising speed, switched the topic.

"I have a sensational idea..." Szaba leaned toward her, taught as a coiled spring. To ease his tension, she rubbed his shoulders and kneaded the surprisingly strong muscles. He went on, "The body parts. What's to stop the company from owning breeding farms in Central America? Impoverished Mestizo women would be fertilized by Yankee sperm...."

"Talk about imperialism!"

"There is a precedent, I've read. A Japanese company offers private patients kidney transplants from the Philippines at half the normal price."

"What happens to the Philippine donor?"

"I don't know. And," he said, brushing her objections aside, "they'd be given abortions. The fetuses would be flown here, the inner organs harvested...."

"I despise that word. It reminds me of a potato field."

"And...." he said, eyes boring into hers, "the organs would be rapidly grown in the protein. Imortalex would sell or lease them for future use by the purchaser."

She looked up at him, her short upper lip contributing to her air of innocence. "Someone who needs a new gall bladder, for instance?"

"That sort of thing. The organs would be reserved for the owner. Profits would be enormous."

"And the mestizo girls?"

"They'd be paid. The money would benefit the local economies."

"Suppose the women refused to have abortions?"

"Either they'd respect their contracts, or...."

"What?"

There was silence, a long silence. Szaba, she suspected, wouldn't resort to empty threats. "Would the fetus develop neurologically?" she asked at last.

"Enough to have organs which would then be removed."

"You'd kill them, huh? You play rough, Zig."

"When I must," he said affably.

"Would you be rough with me?"

"I might." He was affable and ruthless at the same time.

The confidence and raw power he exuded intrigued her and she couldn't resist touching him, though fearing he was the devil. Would Lucifer threaten suicide? She didn't think so.

That night, after a champagne dinner, Freddie pursued an inner argument.

Do you think I should?

I think you shouldn't. Most definitely.

Why not?

You know the reasons.

But I sort of desire him.

That's no reason.

It's the only reason that counts.

*   *   *   *

She ended in the sack with Zig. Had she been satisfied? Yes. It felt good. Was she in love with him? Negative. Yet Szaba could advance her career and Freddie could also play rough if necessary.

How rough? She asked herself. As rough as necessary, she answered.

CHAPTER 15

▼

Szaba rented a medical office on the upper East Side as headquarters for clinical trials. Phase I would be an up to three months study with healthy volunteers. If more than a few of them developed side effects, Phase I would be instantly halted.

Freddie tacked notices on Columbia Hospital bulletin boards to recruit the twenty volunteers who had to be middle-aged or older because that would be the target group for ARP.

The volunteers, who included Martha, would be paid $500 each.

The volunteers were screened by the clinical doctor, a Dr. Malcolm Trent, who performed physicals, checked their vital functions and declared them fit.

As Principal Investigator for the study, Freddie met the volunteers in the East Side office. They needed to sign a medical release, a confidentiality statement, and a waiver of liability; all did so. Most of them were ordinary folk but four of them seemed unusual.

Bart, a bricklayer, was a professional guinea pig for experimental drugs. He volunteered when he was unemployed.

"Oh yes," he said, "I've participated in dozens of clinical trials. All I care about besides the money is how well you stick the needle into me."

Freddie assured him a phlebotomist would draw blood.

"A he or a she?"

"A she."

"Good. But not a doctor. They're the worst. Female nurses are more deft. They study the vein more carefully. The one I have in mind did it fine. She had it down to an art form. She understood how a vein moves under the skin. Some women are great! You don't notice it. They get it right the first time. If she's skilled, it doesn't matter what kind of veins you have. They could do it with babies."

"We won't have infants in the study," Freddie said.

"What's the new drug for?"

"That's confidential," Freddie told the bricklayer.

"I'll find out. I always do," said the stocky man.

"How?"

"Somebody talks."

"Not this time," she said. "No one here knows but me."

Martha, however, knew they tested a protein that might extend human longevity. Freddie accepted her into the program at the last moment, when several other recruits dropped out. After she'd passed the physical with flying colors—heartbeat, pulse, blood pressure, skin tone, skeletal mass, all okay—she had to sign a secrecy agreement, as did the other recruits. "I wouldn't blab," she said.

"No."

"Won't the fact that I'm a former heroin user make a difference?"

"Doesn't seem to. The junk has been washed out of your system. And you have an advantage. You're used to needles."

"Yes. At least I didn't get AIDS. Tell you what. Might I take a double amount of the drug for double pay?"

Freddie checked the protocol. The FDS required an experimental drug be tested at its outer limits in some cases, so she went along with Martha's request, though reluctantly.

Of course, Martha could have been swallowing a placebo—cellulose and sugar—in the capsules, also dictated by FDA procedures: the doctor, Freddie and the recruits would not know; the idea was to learn if the capsule could produce imaginary effects—as sometimes happened—but Martha spoke of increased strength and the arthritis pain in her shoulder abated; Freddie was sure Martha received the protein.

The unemployed TV actress thought what she was ingesting was simply miraculous. "I used to run out of gas before the performance was over. Now I finish and I'm rarin' to go again."

And the past-his-prime circus artist, a slender man with a flame-colored pencil of a mustache, he reported, "I was always afraid I'd fall but my now handholds are much better. What is this stuff, anyway?"

"I'm not allowed to tell you."

"Something to do with youthfulness? When I was a kid I was a fine acrobat. Now I will be again." But he didn't sound that confident and she wondered if he needed a chance to prove himself.

And, cautious as always, she asked the acrobat if he'd had another way of earning bread.

The flame-colored mustache bristled with indignation and Freddie recognized from the still-gray hairs that it had been dyed.

"Oh, that." The acrobat, Lester Buford by name, shuffled his delicate feet. "Must we be that honest?"

"Why not?" She smiled. Weren't smiles friendly by definition, a means of showing your intentions weren't hostile? Like shaking hands?

"Okay. I've been arrested for B&E."

"B and E?"

"Breaking and Entering."

"You're a thief?"

"Only when I'm unemployed."

"Such as now?"

"Correct, but sooner or later I'll rejoin the circus," Lester said.

Freddie saw the professional volunteer once more. "My worry was getting angry, punching the physician and being dumped from the program. Now I don't fly off the handle."

Irascibility, another symptom of aging, had tapered off.

Freddie discussed the results with Dr. Trent. "Decreased joint problems, enhanced energy, better eye-hand coordination, improved sensory perceptions…not bad. And there was no toxicity. What is this drug?"

"We call it magic," she joshed.

The outcome was far from final but seemed to establish the drug had no unwanted side effects.

*   *   *   *

Phase II human testing, which began immediately after Phase I, used 100 volunteers, between 65 and 70, who appeared to be aging fast. The study, managed by various CROs, clinical research organizations, involved patient data which had to be carefully analyzed and put into statistics. The drug's effectiveness had to be determined.

"What does 'effectiveness' mean?" Freddie asked the Prof.

"That, given a high dose, the results, randomized and put into statistical terms, the protein performs as we claim it will."

"And if it doesn't?"

"Cross your fingers."

"Kiss our millions goodbye, huh?"

But the preliminary reports from the CROs looked great. Of the volunteers, by medical standards 90 percent had completely ceased to age.

*   *   *   *

As Szaba had been urging, Geoff took a leave of absence from the hospital. He needed to concentrate on his job as president of Imortalex. Freddie threw a farewell party in his office.

The innocent seeming fruit punch had been spiked as Freddie ascertained on tasting it, probably by Mulheran himself.

"Will you miss us, Prof?" a fellow teacher asked.

"No," Geoff said. "I'll be far too busy as a capitalist!"

"Weren't you once a Socialist?"

"I…can't recall." Mulheran cackled.

Freddie was convinced Mulheran was slightly inebriated.

When the other faculty members had departed he removed a half-empty bottle of vodka from his desk and began drinking in earnest. They were alone.

"What's the matter?" she questioned.

He looked at her from blurry eyes. "I'm nervous."

"Because?"

"Wall Street. I'm supposed to raise funds. Am I up to it?"

"Of course you are. You're a world-renowned scientist."

Tears trickled down his pink cheeks behind his glasses. "I'm old and forgotten."

"You're hardly old, Prof," Freddie said fiercely. "And you might win a major prize for developing the protein."

Mulheran considered. The security of being a fully-tenured professor had always been his crutch. Now he was about to be tested in the real world of money and wondered if he'd be equal to the task. Perhaps outside the walls of academe he was doomed to fail and Zig hadn't made the job any easier. He managed a smile. "I'll have to visit investment bankers and I'm forbidden to mention the product's name."

"Shit! Szaba's obsessed by security."

"Yes, and ARP isn't as sexy as…."

She interrupted him. "Whatever the protein is called by the bankers, its purpose must be presented as improving health. Delaying aging and improving sexual performance would be extra benefits unofficially."

"Yes. The FDA prohibits drug companies from advertising 'off label' uses. Those other than the approved indication—but they can pursue alternative strategies. They can buy ads that raise awareness of a condition without mentioning a product's name. That should suffice." Mulheran cheered up.

*   *   *   *

After being in the doldrums, biotechnology was hot again. One company, for instance, sold for $100 a share, up from $1, a price/earnings ratio of 15:1. Well, that outfit couldn't hold a candle to Imortalex, with its potentially blockbuster product, Imortalon.

An underwriting firm agreed to handle the IPO (Initial Public Offering) at 11 cents a share, but actually opened at $18 and before the end of the day hit $20. Freddie's $10,000 was now potentially worth millions, but privately held Imortalex stock, under SEC regulations, had to be held for a while.

Rumors of a new wonder drug spread on Wall Street. What the multi-million dollar molecule was intended to accomplish remained obscure but the substance seemed promising and had the makes of a première drug, an oh-my-God product. Iris Dove got "miracle protein" mentioned in *Pharmaceutical Marketing* and medical journals, and a Philadelphia broker who specialized in biotech issues ordered a sizeable number of Imortalex shares subject to FDA approval of the product.

Freddie could see no point in going to Washington and having an argument with Stover and took out her frustration on Zig.

"Suppose it doesn't?" Freddie asked from Szaba's canopied bed.

"Doesn't what?" said Zig from his dressing table. He wore a Chinese silk bathrobe.

"Approve Imortalon."

She stayed in his apartment once a week, trying out the relationship cautiously. It was far from smooth. Szaba lost his temper easily over minor matters. The protein had the opposite effect among the test subjects—the capsules seemed to confer calm, a general sense of well-being—so she couldn't blame ARP. Perhaps he was ingesting less than what she assumed would be the recommended dosage.

On the other hand, Martha took double doses of the protein and so far hadn't, to Freddie's knowledge, shown a propensity to be short-tempered. But perhaps Zig used even more of the magic protein than Martha did, though he refused to tell her. They argued about his lack of candor.

He was saying, "But it shall, I assure you. We...." He always referred to "we", bless him. "We will succeed in Phase II testing. The only real hurdle that remains is Phase III."

"A problem," she said. "We're supposed to cure an illness but even if aging is treated as a disease the test subjects won't grow old fast enough for Imortalon to make a difference."

"You solve the problem," he shouted. "You're the Research Director."

Research. She'd have liked to research what lay behind Szaba's tantrums. Was it the protein or business worries?

"Don't scream at me, Szaba. It ain't alluring."

"I will shout if I like.

"At your risk. Tell me what's upsetting you."

She had a hunch he'd find an excuse. "I'll lay it on the line then."

She flinched as if expecting a blow. "Go on."

"I want us to have a baby."

A baby! Stretch marks on her smooth stomach? Breast feeding? Getting up all hours of the night? Being tied down by responsibilities? Besides she wasn't at all sure Zig and she would last, though she might be willing to try. More or less the words she'd used with Mulheran when he'd asked her to investigate Noah's protein.

"*Us?* Me, you mean. Let's stick with the contraceptives. I'm more interested in my career."

"But women are built to reproduce."

"And the man should be functional..."

His sudden rage reminded her of an epileptic seizure she'd witnessed as a student. Only among the students she had had the courage to insert something between the clenched jaws to prevent injury.

"I <u>am</u> functional," he said angrily. "You're concerned with congenital heart failure."

"It hadn't crossed my mind, until now at least. I just want to work without distractions. Get in bed, Zig."

He cursed in Polish, Freddie knew from the angry lines on his face.

*   *   *   *

For Phase II testing, ads were placed in the newspapers or on bulletin boards at senior citizen centers. The chosen subjects suffered from typical old-age afflictions—high blood pressure, mild arthritis, minor (Type Two) diabetes, osteoporosis, incontinence due to renal disease....Of those who received placebos, Freddie learned privately from a compliant doctor, one had died from an aneurism in the heart, but among those who were given the protein the results were astonishing. Blood pressure went down, osteoporosis receded, people who'd stepped carefully to avoid falling now walked briskly, heads up..."The first time I've window-shopped in years," an old woman told her physician.

Lying about her age, Martha wangled herself into a Phase II study group, she told Freddie at the lab where the rats were still being tested. "I love what the protein does for me," she said to Freddie. "It soothes my nerves."

Freddie was troubled. "I hope you're not becoming dependent on the stuff."

"Addicted to a *protein?*" Martha laughed derisively.

Freddie thought of her father's compulsive trips to Atlantic City.

*   *   *   *

Phase II was meant to define the dosage—two capsules per week seemed sufficient to forestall the symptoms of aging. Beyond that level, the dose might be toxic but it was unnecessary, perhaps dangerous to experiment, although rodents given large quantities of the protein didn't fall ill.

Phase II, which had lasted for months, was rapidly winding down, with Phase III to follow immediately. The protein was to be tested in a nationwide multi-center study, on 1000 people aged 65-85 who needed medical help, sufferers from osteoporosis, thrombosis, severe diabetes, every *"osis"* and *"itis"* Freddie could think of. Word of the miraculous protein had leaked and the centers were flooded with applications.

"It's like Lourdes," Szaba remarked. "Throw away your crutches."

"Maybe there's a way out from testing only old people," Freddie said, glancing through a medical journal which contained an article on Hutchins-Guilford progeria syndrome, a replication of aging. "These are young-old kids. Why wouldn't the protein work for them?"

Hutchins-Guilford progeria syndrome victims—a recessive gene was thought to be the culprit—failed to mature properly. They had the appearance of 70 at 9 years old, when typically they died from heart failure because of low cardiovascular output.

Illustrations showed large, bulging crania, with distended veins, wrinkled skin, slack mouths. Almost saddest of all, these kids had normal IQs and understood how grotesque they appeared.

The condition was extremely rare, Freddie noted.

"Would the FDA permit her to test the new drug on children afflicted with a dreadful disease that caused premature aging?" she said to Stover on the phone.

"You mean the Hutchinson-Guilford progeria syndrome? Why do you ask?"

"Maybe the protein would stop the aging."

Silent for a moment, Stover thought: How different she is from the guys in $2000 pharmasuits with their plastic looking greed smiles. She genuinely wants to help people—she doesn't expect a bonus. She won't contact a senator or congressperson if she's turned down. I'd like to assist her without breaking the rules. He finally said, "We have a category called compassionate research. You'd have to file an amendment to the IND. I'll arrange it but I don't understand how ARP would help."

"The protein might affect their genetic apparatus. That's what the molecule was designed for. But first I'll have to locate the kids. I'll require parental consent, of course."

Freddie called children's hospitals throughout the country and found a small number of progeria cases. She selected several. One lived conveniently in Brooklyn, but the parents denied permission; they feared their child would be exposed to ridicule; a divorced California mother didn't seem to care; a married couple in Salt Lake City prayed their child would be cured.

At company expense, Freddie flew to Los Angeles, went to a well-known children's hospital there, presented her card and asked to see the girl who lived at the hospital. "Mary's shy," the physician warned. "Her mother seldom visits. Progeria's a terrible disease. We would have given her your medicine. Why did you bother to come?"

"I wanted to witness the results."

"Mary is here because she has an aversion to school."

Freddie wasn't surprised. Mary was short, almost a midget; her classmates would have made her life intolerable even without the other abnormalities—receding chin, button nose, bulging forehead, deep facial lines.

"How old is she?" Freddie asked the doctor.

"Eleven. Would you believe it?"

Freddie picked up the child who seemed almost weightless. "Hi, dear. Would you mind if I fixed your hair?"

"No, ma'am."

Freddie said to the doctor, "Could I borrow a comb, a pair of scissors and a mirror?"

"I don't see why not." The doctor told the attendant to bring barber tools and Freddie copied the coiffure she'd received on Mad Av. "Why, she's almost cute," the doctor commented.

"Have you a camera? After I'm gone, take her picture, please." She held up the mirror to Mary's hair. "Like it?"

"Yes'um," Mary gasped.

"Okay. Open your mouth."

Mary revealed tiny teeth and Freddie inserted a capsule into her mouth which Mary swallowed with a glass of water. "Twice a day," Freddie said. "The drug is potent. We should see the difference real soon."

Intensely curious, Freddie spent the night at a hotel and returned to the hospital in the morning. Already Mary's facial lines had begun to disappear.

*   *   *   *

The fibroblast growth factor, Freddie remembered, acted on primitive stem cells and healed wounds as well as mediating bodily insulin and healing damaged nerves. It also made wrinkles vanish. The protein somehow caused the genetic process to reverse—muscle mass and cardiac output could be increased. Mary might achieve normal height and weight and might yet be pretty.

FGF was a once-in-a-century discovery!

*   *   *   *

Next she flew to Salt Lake City. The parents brought their son to the hospital where Willie, 13, was an outpatient. He slumped, as if the weight of his bald cranium with distended blood vessels were too heavy to bear, like a cross.

"Straighten up, son," the plainly-dressed father chided.

"He looks like a gnome," said the mothers. "We pray you can cure Willie."

"I'll try," Freddie said. She patted Willie's head. He tried to bite her. "Another Mike Tyson, huh?" She laughed and removed her hand. "I'd hate to be your dentist," she said, coaxing a smile from the boy. "Okay, Willie, time for your medicine."

Willie cowered. "What is it?" he said clearly. "I hate my pills. They taste awful."

"What does he get?" she asked the doctor.

"Aspirin. That's all we could think of."

"Aspirin won't help."

"And your stuff will?" the doctor said skeptically.

"I hope so." She said to the boy, "This medicine tastes good."

She had planned the move in advance, as she always did. For a drug to achieve maximum effectiveness with children, the child had to be eager to take it; otherwise, the child might unconsciously resist. Willie had to be receptive to the protein.

"Well?" he said.

"Okay. Here's some candy." Brown sugar coated the capsule.

Willie put the capsule in his mouth. "More!"

"Better lay in a supply of brown sugar," Freddie advised the parents. "I believe he'll recover. I'll be in touch."

*   *   *   *

She'd been in contact with Noah and he came to her hotel room. "Thanks for leaving the message you'd be in Salt Lake," he said bitterly. "We haven't spoken in weeks. You don't return my calls."

"I've been busy. You can't imagine *how* busy."

"Why are you here?"

"Business reasons."

"Connected with this Szaba?" he said.

"Yes. He's a philanthropist. He gives mostly to hospitals."

"One in Salt Lake?"

"Uh-huh." Christ, could she ever cease lying?

Greenberg eyed her finger. "You're not wearing our engagement ring."

She suddenly decided to be honest. "Look Noah, the fact is…."

His lips sagged. "Tell me. Quick."

"Well, I'm sort of infatuated." Had she talked herself into it?

"I guessed. With this Szaba?"

"Uh-huh. At least for the moment."

Noah withdrew a few paces. "Isn't he a lot older?"

"I don't believe he'll age that much. Not for a number of years, at least." She couldn't tell him Szaba was taking the protein.

"What is this, an experiment?"

"I suppose."

"An experiment has to end, sooner or later."

"Maybe."

"Okay. I'll wait."

"No. Don't do that either, please," she said.

Noah openly cried when he left. Freddie felt sad. She wondered if she'd made the right decision. But there was no turning back. Freddie's heart lay with Imortalon, her true love.

The problem was, she couldn't make love to a capsule.

"Listen! I told you I thought you were lying. Now I'm convinced. You never intended to wear my ring, much less marry me. For all I know I'm being gypped on the protein."

Freddie stayed silent and Noah's tone softened.

"I want to help. It seems to me you might be in a jam."

"Perhaps, but how could you help?"

"Come back from Salt Lake City and confront the bastard."

"Don't do that—yet."

Soon, perhaps.

PART III

▼

ANTI-AGING

CHAPTER 16

▼

Before-and-after photos of Mary and Willie arrived in New York. Only weeks had passed since the kids had started to take the protein and the difference was enormous; they appeared almost normal and would soon be back in school.

Deeply pleased, Freddie showed the photos to Iris Dove who became ecstatic. "The pictures demand publicity."

"So parents of progeria children will realize there's hope," Freddie said.

"Yes and to spread the name of the company. No one's heard of us but now they will!"

Iris secured releases from the parents and the photos aired on TV. Newspapers and magazines ran articles. Queries came from doctors who wanted to know what the kids had been given. "A magic protein," was all the p.r. lady was permitted to say.

There was silence from Imortalex which still waited for FDA approval, but Ted Stover informed Freddie that the results of Phase III testing, which had showed zero negative effects, hadn't been objected to by the IRB. The New Drug Application, now including plans for marketing, would probably be approved by the FDA and in record time. "Break out the champagne," Zig shouted.

While Szaba was fetching the champagne Iris said to Freddie, "I want to kiss you."

"Because you feel euphoric?"

"Whatever that means. Because you're sexy."

"You're thrilled by the FDA's decision?"

"By you."

"Let me get this straight. You find women sexually attractive?"

"Don't you?" The p.r. lady said with a sort of pout. She licked her lips.
Freddie stared at Iris. She murmured, "Once in a while."
Iris bent forward but Freddie averted her face as she had with Szaba.
"If you had to choose between Zig and me, which would you pick?" she said.
"Szaba."
"Because he's a man?"
"Because he's the boss. You're more attractive."
"If Zig and I had a dispute. Who would you side with?"
"Depends."
"Oh?"
"Whether you and I have a relationship."
"We should toast," Zig said, entering with champagne.

*   *   *   *

Next, based on Szaba's casual remark, Iris claimed the magic protein offered a
cure for Alzheimer's. The IRB, composed of physicians, promptly objected and
Mulheran, as president of Imortalex, was compelled to issue a judicious press
release.

"The new drug should not be the basis for excessive speculation. It may well
achieve wonders but we cannot responsibly claim to have discovered a cure for
Alzheimer's Syndrome. The most that can be said is that our molecule might
delay the onset of the disease."

Zig was livid. Freddie overheard him tell Veere, who was in the apartment,
"Mulheran's casting aspersions on the product. The bad judgment is typical of a
lush. He must be taken care of. He's making it harder to raise money and the
burn rate is killing me."

Freddie knew what "burn rate" meant, the cost of keeping the company
afloat—thousands of dollars a day to pay for human testing the IRB, producing
the protein, etc. Szaba was plainly worried.

"Okay," Len murmured.

*   *   *   *

Freddie talked to Geoff who seemed depressed. "I've quit drinking," he said.
"Voluntarily?"
"No. On my doctor's orders. He's given me a warning—I might get sick…."
"At least you have the company to occupy your time."

"As a substitute for booze? How I wish. My hands shake even more. To tell the truth, Fredericka, I hate business every step of the way. I miss science, my colleagues and the lab...."

"You made an important find, prof. The magic protein."

"But is it right to meddle with aging? To interfere with nature's laws? he asked.

"What's wrong with people living longer?"

"It might be unnatural. One could force cells to survive when they should not. The nerves that govern eyesight could stimulate the part of the brain where hearing occurs—one might hear in colors."

"What color would you *hear*?" She teased him.

"Black—I'd paint a funeral scene. Perhaps I should have expired."

Freddie wondered if Mulheran had outlived his usefulness to Imortalex. Where was her loyalty?

*   *   *   *

The FDA ok'd ARP-1 which meant Imortalon could be sold and ads appeared in the medical journals.

IMORTALON!

> The first and only medication for people 55 to 70 (older in some cases) to keep them active, healthy, and youthful.
> No side effects. EXTREMELY WELL TOLERATED...

The SEC permitted the stock offering. Imortalex opened at $25 a share and closed at almost $90 when the NASDAQ halted trading. Freddie's $10,000 investment was worth about a million bucks and the company had become solvent.

Imortalex rented a Madison Avenue office and hired a decorator. The sleek chrome-and-glass ambiance seemed nice to Freddie but Geoff was uncomfortable behind his Danish cantilevered desk, on which hundreds of inquiries about the product had been stranded until Iris passed them to Freddie and suggested she appear on TV in her capacity as Research Director.

"How do I look?" Freddie said to Iris.

"Just gorgeous," Iris said.

On CNBC Freddie explained the demographics of prospective Imortalon—buyers—older and affluent, a segment of the population that would increase. Capsules had to be ingested…"

"How often?"

"Twice a week at $75 per capsule or the users would recommence aging at once. A calendar comes with the drug."

"Free?"

"Absolutely."

Users would rarely be sick. Imortalon would be cost-effective. People couldn't afford not to buy the substance because they wouldn't require other prescription drugs.

A telephone caller asked if the major pharmaceutical outfits' products would take a beating. Freddie demurred.

When would Imortalex turn profitable?

When Imortalon was on the market.

Why wasn't it? they asked.

The FDA had just approved the drug.

There hadn't been time to get it into the pipeline to pharmacies. But she could announce that a new product, Rejuvenon, a skin cream, was in the works.

*   *   *   *

The idea had come to Freddie after she'd visited the castle; the large jar with body parts had upset her; the ichthyotic rash had returned. She'd applied the magic protein and the rash almost instantly disappeared.

Rejuvenon's major constituent was the protein which the FDA had already sanctioned. The fibroblast growth factor must have healed the rash.

The best testimonial for Rejuvenon was Freddie herself. She looked lovely on TV, according to the interviewer and Zig.

She went to the Carlyle after the broadcast and Szaba gave her raves. "Fly away with me, my sweet bird!"

"Is that Polish poetry?"

"No. I have first-class airline tickets."

"Oh dear. To where and why?"

"To Paris. We'll stay in my condo near the Louvre. I must meet my backers. I'm desperately short of cash."

"Because of the burn rate, I suppose. You could sell stock."

"The owner of the company bailing out? How would that appear? People would think there's something wrong with our products."

"Okay. To Paris for the weekend," Freddie said.

The flight to Europe proved uneventful, Zig hardly spoke. His condo was consisted of a living room and kitchen with a small bedroom and seemed to have been designed purely for entertainment. The bar was well-stocked and the refrigerator had been filled with delicacies by the housekeeper, Zig explained.

"Parties are chores" he admitted.

Szaba insisted on making love and did so again and again, as though compulsively, until she began to wonder is something was wrong with him. She was exhausted and failed to achieve satisfaction.

They slept. In the morning he was at her once more—his passion seemed abnormal, contrived almost, but failed to arouse her. Perhaps Freddie was partly to blame because her mind was on the bottom line.

She thought of the protein. Yes, by God, Zig was taking too many capsules, but searching his luggage, Freddie was unable to find them. Dreading a confrontation, she decided to wait.

Szaba's gangster friends arrived in the late afternoon from Poland. Three were men, the fourth a woman, dripping with diamonds, and all spoke with heavy accents and slapped Zig on the back.

"You're doing fine," Freddie understood a Pole to say.

"Great," said a fat man.

"To a longer life," said the thin one, toasting with Zig's Polish vodka.

"And lotsa bucks to spend in it," said the sallow man, placing his arm around Freddie's skinny waist.

"Cheers," Zig said. "I hope you brought greenbacks."

The woman clutched her purse and pointed to the sallow man. "He'd better take his hands off the dame. Is she a movie star?"

"My assistant," Szaba said and Freddie looked at him. "My *faithful* assistant. He stared at the sallow man with baleful eyes.

"Careful," Freddie warned.

Szaba said in rapid English, "The woman's got the money. Don't go near the pale guy. He's her boyfriend."

"Surely *you're* not jealous," Freddie said.

"But I am," Szaba screamed.

"Calm down." There was spittle on Szaba's full red lips; Freddie disentangled herself from the sallow Pole and walked across the room.

Szaba followed and slapped Freddie's face. "You deserved that," he shouted.

"I did?"

"Tak!" which meant, she knew, "Yes" in Polish.

Zig raised a fist and Freddie pretended to cower. She assumed she was part of an act designed to impress the Polish gangsters.

They dined at a three-star restaurant. The bejeweled broad opened her purse and Freddie glimpsed a thick wad of new hundred dollar bills.

That night Szaba received gobs of money in cash and pledges; the Paris trip had been a success.

But, back at the condo, he struck her for no apparent reason, as it stung. She felt sorrier for him than herself. He was losing control.

Shit, she thought, he's finally crossed the line. He really has. Next I'll have whip marks on my ass. How do I feel about this? Give me more punishment because I deserve it? Because we're sadomasochists? Well, I'm not. I'd rather die.

I have to break with Zig for hurting me.

*   *   *   *

Freddie refused to see him outside of the office. She concentrated on business. Mulheran gave her a raise through Zig, of course, but she stuck by her guns.

Protein production had been unexpectedly slow and Imortalon still wasn't on the market.

Mulheran worried about the drug's economic aspects. "Do you realize, Fredericka, that ARP would bankrupt Social Security?"

"I hadn't thought of it, no."

"Well, I have. If individuals live so much longer the government will be forced to send checks for an extra century. Congress never envisioned that in its wildest moments."

"They could raise the retirement age."

"To what? 90? 100? 125? Folks would refuse to work for such an extended period. Pension plans would go bankrupt too. The enormous jump in life expectancy and so many retirees could destroy the United States—because of us."

"A side effect we failed to consider."

"People wouldn't be able to afford capital goods—new cars, refrigerators and such."

"Advertising would dry up?"

"Including ours. And fewer people would be able to afford $150 a week for Imortalon."

"But surely the price will skid if we ever get into mass production?"

"With decreased demand? The price might well rise."

"People pay through the nose for HIV medication," she pointed out.

"But AIDS can be fatal."

"Old age isn't a killer?" Freddie laughed bitterly.

"A paradox," Mulheran grumbled. "A drug that works so well few can afford it. Perhaps it would be best if Imortalon didn't reach the market."

"I have a different idea. Let's convince Washington to hike the retirement age."

"How will that be accomplished?"

"We'll give free samples of Imortalon to everyone tied to the government from the President on down. When the officials realize they'll remain youthful, they'll favor raising the retirement age no matter what."

"I don't understand the logic, Fredericka."

"Can't you see?" With the retirement age extended and millions more working, the market for Imortalon is bound to increase. We'll remain in business."

"That's what I'm afraid of," Mulheran said.

But the old man refused to explain.

*   *   *   *

As insurance in case the stock price dipped, she bought her father's farm, giving him lifetime occupancy of the cottage. But he was seldom there: the money enabled him to continue gambling at the low-stakes poker tables in Atlantic City.

"Don't you lose?"

"Sometimes. That's when I stop for awhile. Mostly, though, I about break even, including my expenses. Hotels and meals are cheap and I don't eat much."

"Or drink?"

"Not a lot and only in my room."

"You're celibate?"

"I don't play around. Your mother's memory is enough."

"You'd be better off with a live female."

"I can't afford whores. Who else would have me?"

"Lots of women, dad. You're still an attractive man."

"Since we're being frank, daughter, what about you?"

"I'm also celibate for the moment. But I'm gambling—on the future."

"Me too. I intend to win for a change."

Could he? And what about her?

CHAPTER 17

▼

Herb, an architect she'd hired to help plan a house for the New Jersey land, wanted to know what she had in mind when Freddie could afford to build.

"Big, I think. Four bedrooms, two upstairs, two downstairs. Plus a library—"

"Libary?"

"Library. The word takes two 'r's."

"Oh?"

"And a stable."

"You have kids?"

"No. I'm not expecting one either."

"Why do you need so much space?"

"I want to be able to roam around."

"You must be rich," Herb said.

"Not yet but soon."

Two years had passed since Freddie had lunched with Greenberg. She was thirty, a dangerous birthday: if you didn't know what you wanted then, you might never. A mature woman ought to have her sights set, but she didn't except for the house. Noah was out of her life for good, she presumed, her relationship with Zig on the rocks. She'd bury herself in the company.

*　　　*　　　*　　　*

Imortalex stock took off again because the small quantities of Imortalon that had finally been produced were being snapped up in drugstores, providing much needed cash. And orders for Rejuvenon, which didn't need a prescription, were flooding in, though the skin cream was not yet on the market.

Freddie felt rich—was the feeling deceptive?—and for the first time since childhood financially stable.

But, she gauged, Geoff was vulnerable. A doctor had told him to cease drinking on penalty of death. Vodka was odorless—probably why he imbibed the stuff—so she couldn't detect it on his breath. Like all chronic drinkers, he was careful to disguise the symptoms. His afternoon slur was, well, softer.

"Prof, you're still into the booze!"

Mulheran denied the accusation.

"I think you're buying alcohol."

"No," Mulheran said firmly.

"Remember what the physician told you?"

"Yes," Mulheran said less firmly.

"Are you in denial?"

Geoff covered his pink ears as though to avoid listening.

They were in Mulheran's spacious office at Imortalex. The windows looked down on Madison Avenue. He failed to respond, just nodded at her meaninglessly.

"You're really fucked up, prof."

"A little fucked up, yes."

"So where do you hide the hooch? Under the settee? In the Danish desk? The water cooler? Shit, it could be almost anywhere." The prof maintained silence.

"You might as well put a gun in your mouth and pull the trigger."

"If I die it won't be an accident, Fredericka."

He declined to elaborate.

*   *   *   *

She knew of a drying-out place where they all but locked you up. Geoff would be under supervision and safe there. But he had to agree to go.

Mulheran avoided her during the next few days—maybe he was drying out on his own. She tried to put herself in his mind.

Willpower, goddamit, would do the job.

Just one more drink....No! I refuse. I won't tough a drop under any conditions.

Yeah, yeah.

Martha had been to see Geoff, she told Freddie. She gathered Martha had been to bed with him. The prof had expressed delight as if his final wish had been granted and then fallen asleep, snoring.

But depression was like a black cloud that followed you everywhere; you couldn't escape. Least of all in your apartment where you microwaved supper, watched public television. Informative but….

Channel surfing, you entered the world of popular culture which was strictly for kids. And the baby boomers. How would a top scientist blend in? He couldn't and wouldn't in the corporate universe either.

A misfit.

An alcoholic.

Freddie pictured the black cloud and decided to take the prof from his apartment if only for a stroll. Fresh air would be good for him. She telephoned.

*   *   *   *

Mulheran's voice was hoarse, almost a whisper. "What's the matter?"

"Nothing."

"Truly, Geoff?"

"Well, somebody's been sending gifts."

"Gifts, prof? Of?"

"Vodka, and I couldn't resist, although I tried."

"Are you sick?"

"I believe I am," he said faintly.

Mulheran's apartment was only a few blocks away and she ran there. The doorman admitted her. The prof's door was unlocked as usual and she found him in the bathroom, retching bile and blood.

She dialed 911 and waited with Mulheran's head in her lap. They carried the prof out on a stretcher and Freddie asked the EMS technician, "Is he dead?"

"He's dying from esophageal varices and won't reach the ER alive."

She saw cases of empty vodka bottles on the kitchen floor and recalled Szaba telling Veere to "take care of" that "lush". Her mentor had been murdered, as surely as if he'd been stabbed in the back on Broadway.

She realized if Mulheran was expendable so perhaps was she. Nothing would stand in the way of Szaba's ambitions, except maybe her death.

＊   ＊   ＊   ＊

"Goddamn you," she said to Zig.

"Why?" he said innocently.

"You knew Mulheran had a weakness for alcohol."

"I did? He should be in AA, then."

"*Should have been.*"

Szaba spread his hands in apparent helplessness. "We've lost the president of Imortalex, potentially the largest pharmaceutical house in the world."

"Why are you saying this? Mulheran's dead. Shouldn't you be grieving?"

He rushed on. "At present Merck is first with Glaxo second because of Zantac. But how can an anti-ulcer agent compare with a drug that brings hyperelongated life-spans? We'll out perform both companies."

Grandiosity now. "You're *that* confident?"

"Yes. Provided we can find a suitable replacement."

"And who might that be? Yourself?"

"By no means. I'll keep the position of CFO and CEO but we need a president."

"You can recruit one from biotech outfits."

"I'd rather the job stay in the family. You, for instance."

"I'm not qualified."

"You're versant in drug research and marketing. And you're glamorous. You'll cause a stir—free publicity. Iris Dove concurs. And you'll get a large raise, Freddie, enough to build your dream house. The job will be provisional, of course, depending on your performance."

Whether I follow orders, that is.

Freddie thought of Mulheran. What would he have wanted her to do? Walk out? But protest would accomplish nothing—Geoff couldn't be resurrected. His apparition advised her to forget him and plunge ahead. He'd be her guardian angel.

"Okay," she murmured to Zig. "Thank you. I'll give it my best shot."

So, incredulous, she found herself in a high-rise office with a Danish cantilevered desk, a personal secretary and a view of Madison Avenue. She ordered the manager of the Newark factory to step up production even if it meant shutting down temporarily to install new equipment. Only a trickle of Imortalon had reached the market.

And she told Herb, the architect, to hire a contractor and start work on the mansion, adding a swimming pool and a hot tub. Someday she expected to entertain investors. The prof had been afraid of bankers, but not Freddie. Important People were those you thumbed your nose at.

And Freddie found herself president of a potentially major corporation. She didn't have a board of directors yet, but that would come soon. Meanwhile, she had the ability to hire and fire, to influence corporate leaders and politicians.

*   *   *   *

Noah had phoned from Utah. He couldn't help Freddie at a distance and he'd resigned from the university.

Now he stood in her office. "How will you earn a living?" She noticed his limp had gotten worse. "Perhaps I'll become a postman." He smiled bravely. "I checked on that Willie kid."

"I have too. He's a normal boy now."

"Miraculous. You gave him the protein, yes?"

"Yes."

"And it was my protein, yes?"

"Sort of," she confessed.

"I deserve something, don't I?"

"I suppose, although Mulheran owns the patents. His estate, I mean," she said.

"Poor Geoff. How did he die? The obit wasn't clear on that."

"Alcoholism," she said bluntly. "Esophageal varices, to be precise."

"Nasty," he said.

"Are you?"

"Will I cause trouble? You bet. Unless I'm recompensed for the protein." His eyes behind the wire-framed glasses glittered with determination—he'd undergone a lake change in Utah.

But the company treasury was low on cash. Instead, she offered him stock. "No," Greenberg said. He was inherently conservative. "I don't trust Imortalon. The protein might prove problematic. I'd rather have a job."

Freddie pondered. "You could replace me as research director."

"Where would I be situated?"

"Just down the hall."

Noah's swarthy face wrinkled in thought. "Is there a plug for an electric razor?" His beard was black although he'd shaved that morning, he said.

*   *   *   *

Freddie hoped Noah was satisfied at least temporarily but she soon had Martha to contend with.

Ever since the loose change episode, she'd never really had faith in the woman.

Martha came to Freddie's office complaining of a headache. "I ought to lie down."

Freddie pointed to the couch. "Have you a fever?"

"I don't think so."

"Is it a migraine?"

"I've never had a migraine. Never have headaches for that matter. I feel weird."

In her bathroom Freddie dampened a washcloth and laid it on Martha's brow. "Why the headache? Tension, maybe?"

"I'm not tense."

"Some other reason, perhaps? Miss the lab?"

"I work in the cafeteria again and I'm happy there."

"Mulheran's death must have cast a shadow."

"He and I had a future. I'm glum, that's all."

"So what's wrong, Martha?"

"The protein, I suspect. The testing...."

"The human subjects are fine," Freddie said.

Martha rose to her feet "But I took double doses. Two times the amount than anyone else."

"And you were paid double," Freddie said coldly.

"I should be paid more. A lot more. The protein's given me headaches," Martha howled.

"You lack proof," Freddie remonstrated.

"*I'm* the proof. I'll go on TV news and..."

Anything on Imortalon was a news-catcher. Whole programs had been based on the protein.

LIVE LONGER THROUGH IMORTALON

"We'll dispute your claim. The shoplifting charges won't help you..."

Martha stormed out.

*   *   *   *

As a scientist, Freddie felt obliged to check the facts. Martha could be misusing evidence.

Freddie discussed the accusation with Zig, to whom she spoke as infrequently as possible. "She's a blackmailer," he said.

"I guess. And a thief."

Szaba seemed worried. "She could cast doubt on the safety of the product. She mustn't be allowed to talk."

*   *   *   *

Freddie lunched with Noah and informed him of Martha's headache. "She might be correct," he said.

"What do you mean?"

Noah stared at her. "I warned Professor Mulheran the chimpanzee virus, even if diluted, might conceivably cause severe headaches."

"She might be faking them. The virus *can't* be in the protein."

"I'm sorry to tell you—I checked with the Centers for Disease Control—but some viruses attach themselves to protein receptors. And she had double doses of the protein grown in the virus. A physician ought to examine her," Noah said.

Noah picked up the tab, reluctantly.

Freddie failed to understand why Mulheran had claimed the simian virus wasn't harmful when Noah had warned him it might cause headaches. Maybe even the lab animals had suffered from them. How could the prof have been so badly wrong?

She put herself in Geoff's place. Perhaps Mulheran had deliberately minimized the risks in his enthusiasm for discovery; if the new protein proved a breakthrough, a prize and riches might result; personal objectives had superseded scientific skepticism and, after all, a biohazard was only "conceivable".

She had to blame the human element for Geoff's faulty judgment. All of us make mistakes.

＊   ＊   ＊   ＊

Freddie phoned Martha to come to the office that evening. Dr. Trent would be there.

"I don't recall the individual," Trent said.

"Part of the test group."

"There were hundreds of them. Well, she's late," Trent said. "Not too late, I hope. I'm leaving for vacation early tomorrow."

"She took the subway. That must be the reason."

Martha finally showed, in tears. "Somebody on the subway pricked me with a pin."

"A pin?" Freddie asked.

"Or a needle. In the back."

"Was it a kid?"

"I don't know. The car was crowded."

Freddie imagined the scene: dark car, gleaming needle with a globule on the end buried between Martha's thick shoulders.

"Let me see," Trent said. Martha pulled up her blouse. Trent scowled. "A puncture wound." Freddie looked too. "Isn't it a bit swollen?"

"Maybe a little. Must have been a prank."

The thought of Carlos, never far from her mind, made Freddie intensely suspicious. "She should be checked at a hospital as a precaution."

"Columbia," Martha said, and shivered.

"I'll drop you off in a cab? It's on my way home," Freddie said.

"Nothing serious," Trent said. "How's the headache?"

"Ghastly," Martha moaned.

Columbia insisted Martha remain overnight for observation.

＊   ＊   ＊   ＊

Next day, Freddie learned from the hospital Martha was seriously ill with meningococcal meningitis and ran a high fever.

The disease was infectious and Martha was in isolation, so Freddie wasn't allowed to visit her.

The day after that, Martha died.

Because of the puncture wound, her body was brought to the NYC morgue to be autopsied.

."You ought to pay particular attention to the brain," Freddie suggested over the phone to the deputy coroner, thinking of the headaches.

"Of course," the woman promised. Was she for real?

CHAPTER 18

▼

DEAD WOMAN STOLEN FROM MORGUE
Police Find Body in East River

"Her name was Martha Brown…." Freddie read in a daily paper. Her heart sank. Had they performed the autopsy? She dialed the deputy coroner.

"Is it true?" she cried.

"And that's not the half of it. What the paper didn't tell you was that Martha had been decapitated."

"Oh my God. By who?" She visualized Martha's double chin.

"A ghoul. The perp made it seem like she'd been assaulted by a necrophiliac to confuse us—her labia had been slashed, but there was no penetration…"

"How'd he take her from the morgue?"

"We haven't the foggiest."

Freddie had saved the ultimate questions. "Did you do the autopsy?"

"The body was gone before we could incise the head."

No cranial pop for Martha then. Pressure in the brain caused the skull to make a loud sound when it was sawn open.

She summoned Noah.

"Now we'll never know whether Martha had contracted the monkey bug," he said.

"They would have found brain lesions? Something like that?"

"Absolutely."

She thought of Veere. And Szaba. He really was a bastard, a murderer. She'd have to take action against him, sooner or later. Zig could have bought the meningitis germ on the black market, maybe abroad. Martha had been sacrificed—literally lost her head—so proof of Imortalon's possible danger could be suppressed. Freddie fought back tears.

"Martha's medical records—they ought to contain relevant information," she said.

"About headaches? Prior to the onset of meningitis?"

"Yes. Although Martha wouldn't have been permitted into the human testing program if she'd displayed such symptoms," Freddie declared.

Noah said alertly, "She must have developed the headaches after the human testing was completed."

"Dr. Trent might know. He was the attending physician for the human studies. Martha might have gone to him since he wouldn't have charged her. He'd have billed the corporation."

"I'll call Trent," Noah said, "since I'm research director."

They were in Freddie's Imortalex office as she pressed buttons immediately. The doctor was on vacation but Noah spoke with his assistant who didn't recall Martha. "Our office handles hundreds of patients," Freddie heard him say over the speaker phone.

"She complained of persistent headaches," Noah said. "The point is, we need to know when they began."

Freddie reasoned: If Martha had headaches just before the testing started then Protein X was not responsible, but it might have been after Martha ingested double doses of ARP, grown in monkey virus.

"What was her last name?" the assistant said.

Noah looked at Freddie who said, "Brown. Martha Brown."

"I'll check the computer….No record of Martha Brown or Brown Martha. But our office must have sent you a bill for the visit."

The Imortalex computer had no record of Martha either.

"Shit," Freddie said. "The bill would have included Martha's recent medical history. It has to be somewhere, maybe logged under the rubric 'Human Testing'."

Greenberg worked the computer. "No."

"The file cabinets then. They're in Szaba's office down the hall. He's at the dentist."

Noah limped on the thick carpet but the paper chase was in vain.

"Maybe he keeps the records in his apartment," Freddie said.

"I'll come with you," said Noah.

"That would arouse curiosity. The Carlyle is just up the street. I'll walk." She had to hurry and poor Noah would be too slow.

The doormen knew her and she had a key. Nobody was in the apartment. She flicked on Zig's computer and searched for Brown, Martha, Martha Brown. Nothing. She remembered the cartons in which the animal records had been stored. Maybe Martha's records were in them. She'd left the cartons in a closet but they were gone.

To the factory?

$$*\qquad*\qquad*\qquad*$$

Zig appeared, a wild expression on his face. "Why are you here?"

"I knew sooner or later you'd return from the dentist."

"You wanted to comfort me?"

"Oh yeah. Sure."

"Where?" Szaba laughed sardonically. "In the bedroom?"

"Listen, Zig. You wore me out in Europe. I'm sore."

"The protein gives me extra energy."

"I *thought* you were different. You're taking the capsules?"

"Mmmmmmmm."

"You didn't bring them to Paris. I searched your luggage."

He stared at her solemnly. "I had one in my shaving kit. And we were only there two nights."

"*Only* two? I'm afraid you're becoming dependent on the protein."

"An ARP abuser?" he mocked.

"Hooked." As Mulheran had been on alcohol and her father was on gambling. "No."

"Prove it then. Get rid of the capsules."

"I shall. First let's visit the bedroom."

"Not until I've inspected Martha's medical records."

"Martha?" he said calmly. "Why are you concerned with her? She's dead."

"That's the reason I'm concerned. How do you know she's dead? The newspaper?"

"The hospital advised me."

Yes, he would have phoned to be certain Martha had succumbed to the meningitis Veere had given her in the subway. Then he'd instructed Veere to hijack the corpse from the morgue, with Mark's help. It must have happened in the dead of night and bribery must have been involved. Then they'd cut off the head and dumped everything in the river. The cranium, being small, would never be located. Freddie dealt with maniacs, had to be careful not to be the next victim.

"Okay."

"Why do you want Miss Brown's records?"

"I was checking for possible side effects from ARP as the FDA insisted."

"Well," said Szaba, "she's deceased."

"I guess that's right. The records don't matter much now. To hell with them."

*   *   *   *

She left, promising to the return, but she had to look in the factory for the records. It would have been the perfect place for Szaba to hide them, she told Noah.

"I'll go," he said.

But she couldn't permit him to travel alone and confront Veere with his knife, needle and other toys.

"Let's drive there," she said with foreboding.

"You have a car?"

"Leased to the company."

Things had changed dramatically since she'd been to Newark with Zig in the Daimler. The warehouse, freshly painted, had small, frosted-glass windows that couldn't be seen through, admitting the light but giving no indication of what went on inside. The only clue was a small, tasteful sign over the stuccoed entrance: IMORTALEX.

The parking and shipping area lay in the rear. It would have to be expanded once they got into full production. Fortunately, the plant had been designed to permit duplication of the existing product line, but manufacturing the drug was as yet extremely slow: keeping the tank at the proper temperature had been the difficulty; the quality-control engineers had rejected many samples as contaminated or containing insufficient protein to meet FDA standards.

The customers had to receive the exact labeled amount of ARP to stop aging, the company pharmacovigilance chemists advised.

By then, Imortalex had grown so fast it was hard for Freddie to keep track of the pieces.

To say nothing of the retreats Szaba had organized. Imortalex groups received the age-delaying product before the drugstores. Cameras weren't permitted behind the concertina wire of the enclosures and Freddie had yet to inspect one.

She had read in the company newsletter glowing accounts of an 80-ish Pan, bald head surrounded with grapes, a fig leave over his groin, followed by white-haired nymphs with perfect figures to parties that would last all night. No wonder the codgers clamored for membership!

Iris Dove planted column items: For sheer excitement, you can't beat Imortalon communities. The thrill of staying younger…undying romance…perpetual love….

Zig was right, according to projections. Imortalex would become a pharmaceutical colossus. Every week the stock reached new heights.

Yet the computer refused to admit her when she presented her face to the visiplate. "Your name," the automated voice repeated.

"I told you. Freddie Ferguson."

"Insufficient data."

"Fredericka then."

Silence. She imagined the DC stun guns rising on metallic wands from their cradles.

"No authorization for Fred-er-ick-a Fer-gu-son."

"I'm president of the company, for shit's sake."

Another silence. Noah said, "The computer is stupid."

"I think it's programmed for delay."

After a long moment, the voice said, "You may proceed, Dr. Ferguson."

"I think it recognized your cussing," Noah joked.

Noah offered his face to the visiplate. "Who is this man?"

"Noah Greenberg, research director."

"Insufficient information."

"What the fuck," Freddie growled.

The steel door to the interior swung open with a pneumatic cough.

Len Veere looked up from a desk in feigned surprise.

"Ms Ferguson," he said respectfully. "Why are you here?"

Freddie squared her shoulders. "I want to inspect the facility."

"Shouldn't you wait for Mr. Szaba?"

"He's expected then?"

"Any minute now."

Untrue. Even if Zig had been alerted as to their presence, an hour would be required for him to arrive in the limo. They had sixty minute's grace and would make the most of them. "Let us look at the factory," Noah said.

Veere frowned. "There's not much to see. The freezer where we store the virus, the tank we heat the protein in, the machine that fills the capsules…"

"Don't you have a library?" Noah asked, "with medical records?"

"No," said Veere.

"How about a storage area?" Freddie said.

"No."

"A place where you keep old records?"

"Well...."

"Show us," Noah insisted.

They mounted to the second floor which contained the freezers and the manufacturing equipment. Noah trailed behind. Veer pointed to a narrow ladder. "Nothing up there but cardboard boxes and I doubt if *he* can climb the ladder."

"But I can," Freddie said.

On her cheerleader's legs she scrambled up, pushed a panel aside and hoisted herself. She switched on the single light bulb and spotted the cartons.

"Who brought the boxes here?" she called.

"Mark, Mr. Szaba's driver," Veer said slowly.

These were the right cartons then. If Zig had chosen to hide Martha's records he couldn't have found a better place. He had to be able to locate Martha's testing history in case of a lawsuit. Ultimately the records would be destroyed. She searched the tops of the boxes and finally found a scrawled "S", as on the card attached to the orchids, years ago it seemed.

Martha's records were on top but Freddie lacked the time to read them. She shoved the pages under the front of her skirt and scrambled down.

"Nothing of interest," she said to Veere.

"Okay, we can leave," said Noah.

"You drive," she said to him. "Hurry."

She feared Zig would come—well over an hour had passed.

She spotted the silver Daimler as they turned into the avenue. The limo was headed fast down the street where the factory was and she scrunched down in the car, though Szaba wouldn't know what kind of car she'd leased.

After they were out of sight of the Daimler, she extricated the pages from her midriff and started to read:

IMORTALON
CONFIDENTIAL
HUMAN TESTING PHASE I

PATIENT'S NAME: BROWN, MARTHA, AGE, 49. HEALTH EXCELLENT AT COMMENCEMENT OF STUDY. As Phase I continued, the clinical physician received complaints from the patient. She suffered from continual headaches, at first mild, then severe. The physician ordered her to stop ingesting double doses of Protein X and to report the symptoms to the Principal Investigator but the patient refused, mentioning an urgent need for money. She then denied the headaches continued and referred the physician to Professor Mulheran, who referred him to a Mr. Szaba, who insisted the drug was safe. Mr. Szaba cited the animal studies..../s/Malcolm Trent, MD, Ph.D., Clinical Physician.

So! Dr. Trent must have been rewarded by Zig to ensure his silence. And she remembered what had happened to the rhesus, the beagle and the mare.

No toxicity, eh? Extremely well tolerated....

A conspiracy had secured FDA approval.

She turned to Noah. "Might there be a cure for the monkey virus infection?"

"No."

"Tell me flat out. The purpose of the magic protein—anti-aging—could become less important than the side effect?"

"Uh-huh."

"Who wants to live almost forever with an unspeakable headache? Myself, I'd rather be dead."

"Okay."

"But Martha took twice the basic quantity of the protein than the other subjects, and they didn't report headaches," Freddie cried. "The protein must be safe in relatively small amounts."

"Maybe," he said cautiously. "But the substance could build up in body tissues over time."

"Like fat."

"Exactly."

"So there *is* a danger."

"I'm not sure. Maybe you should wait before you act."

"Until?"

"Something happens," he said vaguely. "When more data is available, we can make recommendations based on facts. Perhaps there's a threshold for the headaches that's dose-dependent. Perhaps the lower doses would take longer to cause the side effect. Who knows?"

"Let's try on another possibility for size. Suppose the monkey virus blocks the anti-aging protein. Wouldn't you age fast, as though the body wants to return to its pre-Imortalon condition?"

"You'd have an old-age epidemic," Noah said.

CHAPTER 19

▼

When they met next day at the office Szaba was crimson with rage.

"You went to Newark!"

"I needed to check on production."

"And you brought this Greenberg."

"What's wrong with that? He works for us."

"You climbed into the loft. Why?"

She laughed. "I needed the exercise."

"You were snooping around, Freddie. What were you after?"

"Records," she confessed.

"Which records?" he hissed.

"The rat studies," she lied.

"Not Martha's?"

"No," she said in feigned surprise.

"Why the animals', for God's sake?"

"I wanted to recheck their diets. It occurred to me the protein might have affected their metabolism, they ate so much. And yet the rodents failed to gain weight."

"Aha," he said. His hands stopped shaking; his expression changed to placidity. "Perhaps we should manufacture a diet product based on ARP."

"Haven't we enough on our plates with Rejuvenon?" She said cheerfully. "Where is the skin cream to be produced?"

"I've found a place in New Jersey." He paused and then said with renewed anger, as if the mere mention of New Jersey reminded him of Noah. "Are you flirting with Greenberg?"

"I wouldn't describe our relationship as flirtatious. Anyhow, you have no right to be jealous."

"Don't I? I still adore you, Freddie."

"And I'm on edge." She remembered Martha who'd lost her head in the East River. Sooner or later, she hoped, she'd avenge the woman.

Almost incoherently, Zig grumbled. "Got to be rid of Greenberg…Don't want him…Yes, I'll…."

"Look, Greenberg's a valuable employee."

Freddie feared Szaba might have a stroke. Or go berserk. It had to be the capsules. How bizarre! The founder of the company addicted to his own product. "Zig, stop taking the capsules…I warn you."

"No," he declared.

"But the drug might cause you to get instantly older than you were when you started taking the capsules."

"A real bad fantasy, Ms Ferguson."

✱   ✱   ✱   ✱

Noah limped into Freddie's office a few days later. "I've been dismissed," he said.

"Summarily? Without notice?"

"I must clear out at once."

"Severance pay?"

"Nothing. I wasn't here that long."

"Does your medical insurance go with you?"

"They canceled the policy."

"It's like a reprisal."

Noah said with bitterness, "I've only tried to help. What went wrong?"

"Me," Freddie said. "I shouldn't have brought you to Newark. Szaba's fit to be tied."

"So am I. Have you seen this?"

He whipped out a business daily column from his jacket—he'd begun to dress fashionably—and showed her a paragraph circled in black marker. It asserted Greenberg had been fired from his post at Imortalex because of malingering: he was frequently found at a country club playing tennis.

"You can't play tennis," Freddie exclaimed.

"I wish I could."

"Are you a member of a country club?"

"Of course not."

"Iris Dove must have planted the item." Freddie pounded her chic desk. "They'll be sorry."

"Well, actually I'm sorrier," Noah said.

"How will you support yourself? Can I give you a loan?"

"I don't care to be in debt. I'll find something, maybe a government job. They hire cripples, I've heard; an Equal Opportunity Employer."

Noah struggled to his feet.

*   *   *   *

Freddie marched to the Carlyle, furious. What business did Szaba have to disregard her wishes? Was she only a figurehead, like Mulheran? No, goddamit. She'd lay it on the line, establish her authority. Maybe Greenberg could be reinstated.

Zig was home with the corporate attorneys she'd met before. He embraced her warmly as always, but seemed downcast. "We're being sued, my dear."

"By?" she asked.

Zig sighed and faced the lawyers. The taller one, a paunchy man named Welsh, said, "By Minerva Neurosciences, owned by Japanese, based in Boston."

"Weren't the scientists who advised us from Boston?" she asked Zig.

"I should never have trusted them. What is the lawsuit for?"

"Patent infringement," Digby, the other lawyer, chimed in. He was short and thin. Both wore ties and suits, while Szaba was clad in his velvet smoking jacket. "They claim to have developed a similar molecule before we did."

"A molecule from Australia," Welsh said.

"There are a lot of molecules," Szaba explained to the lawyers who listened deferentially. "A fingernail of dirt may contain between fifty and a hundred million living organisms representing three or four thousand species. Microbiological colonies are in a constant state of chemical war—like the pharmaceutical companies. Does this action have merit?"

"Well, Minerva's molecule is also a protein," Digby said. "They've established the structure with x-ray crystallography. It's surprisingly close to ARP and they've applied for a patent. They assert Professor Mulheran stole their formula."

"Geoff?" Freddie gasped. "He might have made mistakes but theft wasn't among them."

"How can you be sure?" Digby asked.

"Well, his character."

"He was an alcoholic. I've learned," Welsh said and looked at Szaba.

"So?"

"That tells you about his character," Welsh said sourly.

Freddie recalled how hard the prof had worked! Even though, she had to admit, he may have erred badly on the monkey virus. But his intentions had been honorable and his memory shouldn't be impugned. "I'll deny in court Geoff was guilty of anything," she said.

"That won't matter," Digby said.

"Minerva has influence. Its motto, *Veritas…*"

"Truth," Welsh interjected.

"…is the same as Harvard's. In fact, Minerva may be affiliated with Harvard," Digby said. "They almost can't lose."

"How much are they suing for?" Freddie said.

Welsh rolled his eyes. "Don't ask."

"Enough to bankrupt Imortalex," Szaba said stolidly. "Our legal fees alone will be in the millions…."

"Settle," the short attorney advised.

"Out of court," said his paunchy counterpart.

"I…we…don't have the dough," Szaba said. "The rotten bastards."

"Won't Minerva have legal costs as well?" Freddie said.

"Yes. But we might be liable for them if Minerva wins," Digby said.

"The case could drag on for years," Szaba complained. "It might interfere with our main product, Imortalon."

"But we have Rejuvenon as a resource."

"I'm not certain of the product's potential. So many competitors," Szaba explained. "With Imortalon we don't have serious ones."

"No," said Welsh. "You have the turf to yourself."

Freddie rubbed her cheek and reflected. The rash had vanished, seemingly forever, but Imortalon represented a serious scientific challenge that she hoped to surmount. Maybe Imortalex, Inc. didn't really need Rejuvenon, she said.

"What?" Szaba questioned sharply.

"Well, you—we—haven't invested much in the cream yet. Maybe we should give it to Minerva in exchange for their dropping the lawsuit."

"Unthinkable," Szaba said. He paused, "The suit is utterly without merit, you say?"

"Not utterly," Digby admitted. "And Minerva has clout. Who knows what a judge would believe."

"Well…" Szaba said to Freddie, "But Rejuvenon's your brainchild."

"I suppose I can exist without it."

Welsh went to the phone and murmured. At last he signaled Digby. "We have ourselves an arrangement," the attorney said.

*   *   *   *

In the excitement, she had forgotten Noah's plight, Freddie realized as she hurried back to the office. But, without Rejuvenon, which he'd been testing, he'd have little to do there. Maybe he'd find a better job; he ought to forget her and she him.

After all, she hadn't fallen in love with Noah and at this rate never would. Better to leave men out of her life.

But she couldn't forget the protein. ARP might cause severe headaches but how could she be sure? Martha's case history was inconclusive. Maybe Freddie had overlooked something in the animal studies. They were at the factory, however.

That afternoon she had to approve the latest ads for the product. Iris Dove showed them.

Healthy, wealthy and wise
Then IMORTALON's for you

"Maybe," Freddie said...

Life expectancy may be doubled with
IMORTALON
Excellent health and vigor assured

"Perhaps," Freddie said. "Insert 'almost entirely' before 'assured'."

IMORTALON
Guarantees a longer, fuller life in every sense

"Sense?" Freddie asked.

"Sex," Iris said.

"Those agency people got carried away," Freddie said. "I only like the first one. It doesn't exaggerate too much, though I'm troubled by the 'healthy'."

"Whaddya mean? You got something against health?" Iris said.

It's just that...oh, never mind."

The headaches haunted Freddie. They were like a signal that Imortalon should be withdrawn before it had saturated the market. She was now convinced that, in time, the magic protein would have serious side effects. But how could she validate or invalidate the theory?

Szaba? Yes, he'd ingested far too many capsules.

If they failed to make him suddenly age without headaches, the magic protein was okay to ingest.

Freddie *had* to stop thinking about Imortalon.

"Tell me, Iris, does Zig pay you well?"

"Very well."

"Including overtime?"

"Whaddya mean?"

"I think you understand."

"Take me for a whore?"

"Maybe a high-priced call girl."

"Listen, Freddie, I've got a job."

"You could do it on the side."

"Like you?" Iris sneered.

Freddie laughed, "I'm better paid."

"You haven't heard the end of this," Iris said sadly.

The value of Imortalex stock shot up after the ads appeared. Her purism had been naïve, Freddie had to admit. It was good to be rich.

CHAPTER 20

▼

The price of Imortalex stock had increased 1000 percent and Freddie sold a number of shares. She could not be accused of trading on insider information: she had none. The news on Rejuvenon had already been in financial journals and as for Imortalon, the future was out of her reach.

Her accountant placed her net worth at nearly four million dollars—more than enough to build the house—but the money didn't count nearly so much as product safety.

She resolved to confront Szaba. Once and for all. Was he hooked on the protein simply because it made him feel young? How much had he taken? Did he suffer from skull-wrenching headaches as a side effect? Or was he all right?

Despite herself she worried about Zig. He might hold within his body scientific secrets of the monkey virus. Had it unhinged him? Was that the reason he'd struck her? Should she forgive him on medical grounds? Or was there nothing to apologize for? Perhaps she'd exaggerated as Mulheran was sometimes guilty of.

*   *   *   *

On her way home, having worked late one evening, she impetuously stopped at the Carlyle. The doorman didn't bother to announce her and she keyed herself in. Szaba's head swiveled. "What are you doing here?"

"I wanted to surprise you."

Zig wore a terry-cloth bathrobe. "Why? I never grasp your motives."

She stood, lips apart, conscious of being an attractive woman with a sexual aura who had rejected him. She had to learn the truth, but was suddenly struck dumb by timidity.

"Come on, talk," he demanded

"Zig, are you *that* afraid of aging?"

He forced himself to smile it seemed to her, a crooked smile, almost rueful, as if to say, 'Here I am, no more than middle-aged, but already long-sighted and short-winded, more or less toothless, though I have implants, incapable of strenuous physical exertion (Mark, my nitwit chauffeur, is my surrogate), my memory is not as keen as it was, my hearing's dulled, especially in the right ear, my balance is off, my hands less sure, my lungs wheeze, my potency's up for grabs without the aid of chemicals.'

She received his message as if through an invisible microphone. Perhaps he spoke, perhaps not. She felt hypnotized. At last he said, in a clear voice, "Yes, I guess I am."

"Are you really addicted to ARP?"

Szaba said mildly, "You know I use the protein."

"Abuse the stuff. How much do you take?"

"A considerable amount."

"Do you have severe headaches?"

"Sometimes." He blinked.

"How do you bear the pain?"

"Easy. Sedatives."

"As ARP accumulates in your system you'll need ever-stronger pills," she warned.

"A small price to pay for immortality."

"For you, maybe, but how about others?"

Szaba shrugged, an indifferent gesture. "I don't give a damn for others. Let them eat aspirin. They'll be alive and sexually potent. For most, those are the paramount goals."

"Breathing and fucking? Are those mature objectives?"

"As far as I'm concerned."

"And dreadful headaches."

"They'll suffer in silence." His voice rose.

"Or sue. Or commit suicide. Imortalon must be removed from the market."

"And ruin my future?" Szaba said loudly.

"Look, Zig, you won't have a future. You'll be so old the only future will be in the past."

"Meaning?"

"Taken to excess, ARP causes one to renew the aging process at a very rapid rate. You'll be older than you were already."

Spittle appeared on Szaba's lips and he seemed extremely agitated. "I'd prefer death."

"Whose?"

"Yours."

He didn't seem hostile; it sounded like a simple statement of fact.

"You're insane, Zig. Tell me where you keep the capsules." She intended to destroy them.

"In the bedroom but it's presently occupied."

"By?"

The answer emerged—Iris Dove. Shoe wore a nightgown and had perfume between her breasts, Freddie's nose detected.

Iris, who just a few nights ago had said, 'You haven't heard the end of this.' Iris' revenge. Yes.

Freddie kept calm.

Her lack of jealousy appalled her. Was she devoid of emotions? Was she, indeed, made of steel? Had she ever loved Szaba? No, she despised him, although she still had to save him from himself. For scientific reasons, of course.

Not personal ones. Not any longer.

Iris said in a small voice, "Will I be fired?"

Szaba shook his head.

"Not by me," Freddie said.

She marched into the bedroom but found only a few capsules. Where did Zig stash them? Not at the factory, though they must have originated there. The premises were regularly searched for contraband Imortalon which would bring a hefty price on the black market. Boxes of the drug were carefully counted before being shipped.

The question remained: where did Zig keep the protein? Someplace secure. Why hadn't she thought of the castle?

*   *   *   *

Early next morning she drove to Great Barrington and up the hill. No cars were parked in front of the tall white building which probably meant the summer tenants hadn't arrived. She put her car behind the house, just in case.

She jimmied a window and crawled in. She ransacked the place, finding nothing. The protein had to be in the underground chamber, behind the brass-studded portal.

How could she gain access? She pushed the door with all her might, knowing it was futile, and then tried inserting a credit card behind the latch. The trick failed, however. About to give up, she turned the handle, and the door opened.

Mark must have been there, forgotten to lock up. She donned the goggles and entered the chamber.

Months had passed since she'd been there. The body parts in the huge jar, bathed in the bubbly nutrient, had grown even more.

She found the protein powder in a barrel. Also, a large supply of capsules and a machine for filling them.

She might have crushed the capsules and upset the barrel but Szaba would easily replace them. Imortalon would soon be widely available. The public should be protected from side effects and addiction.

Mark shambled in. Uh oh.

His white hair glowed in the fluorescent light; the key ring was visible between his rounded shoulders which, with his long arms, formed a U against the bubbles. Freddie pressed herself against the wall, hoping Mark wouldn't notice her presence. Up close, he was larger than she had thought.

He bent, poured protein powder from the barrel into the machine, using a ladle, and with surprisingly deft fingers, inserted the capsules which were automatically filled.

He couldn't have spotted her. Maybe she should tiptoe from the crypt while he was preoccupied. On quiet feet she padded out but his goggles lifted and his eyes blinked in startled recognition. He reached for her with a tentacle-like arm and she jumped back, jostling the container.

She spoke to him as if he were a dog. "Down, boy."

Mark frowned and she thought, I've said the wrong thing. I'm a goner for sure. What will he do to me? She was beyond fear, into the dark domain of sheer terror.

Angry and frustrated, she seized the large key ring around Mark's neck and jammed it over his sloped shoulders until it pinioned the arms.

There! She had only to make a run for it. But Szaba yelled from just outside, "Mark! The capsules!"

He must have paused to take the goggles from the hook but she remembered only two pairs and she and Mark wore them. Zig would be blind if he came in and she went outside to confront him.

"You!" he said, voice reedy like a clarinet.

She was shocked by his appearance. Pouches hung from beneath his eyes, his cheeks were lined, his hands shook. My God, he'd aged twenty years overnight!

"The protein," he clamored, snatching for her goggles. She held them aloft—he was too weak to struggle. She considered tripping him and stomping on his head. Maybe he'd die and she'd be rid of him. If he lived, he wouldn't remember.

But Freddie wasn't capable of homicide, not yet. Some day, perhaps. In the meantime, she'd do her best to go along with Zig,—she had no choice. She handed him the goggles and he staggered into the crypt.

Freddie watched in horror from the doorway as he grabbed a fistful of protein and shoved it into his mouth. Almost immediately he stopped shaking.

He freed up Mark who placidly returned to packing capsules.

Zig came back outside. The pouches and deep facial lines were rapidly vanishing, the skin smoothing, his voice had already returned to normal. "Explain yourself."

"I….wanted to stop you from taking the protein."

"Impossible."

"It made you age."

"Temporarily. Because my system got out of whack. I'll live until the end of the twenty-first century, maybe into the twenty-second. If my vital organs fail, I have substitutes." He pointed at the phantasmagoric shapes in the container.

"Listen, I can't help but worry, Zig. Who could? We have a product on the market that might be not only habit-forming but bring about premature aging if taken to excess."

"Imortalon's a prescription drug. Doctors won't allow people to have too many capsules."

"Forget the physicians. Folks will break into pharmacies if they have to."

"Let's go upstairs for some port, Freddie."

She followed him, pretending to be compliant, hoping against hope he regretted Martha's murder and wouldn't attempt the same with her. He appeared panicky so she didn't think he would. But beyond doubt, Zig had become a full-fledged addict.

She glanced back at Mark, still at work with the machine. And then she had it. For Zig immortality transcended everything. He thought he had defeated at last man's ancient enemy, death. Compared to that, Martha's murder was unimportant. Besides, where was the proof?

Szaba ladled dark wine from the keg. He raised his crystal glass. "To longevity."

"To shit," she said. "I'm trying to invent another slogan for the drug. *Live longer but you'll instantly age from Imortalon, an addictive substance*," she toasted bitterly. "Doesn't that sum it up? Except for the headaches. How are yours?"

"Tolerable."

"Look, Szaba, I must file a serious adverse event report with the FDA. Maybe, if used in moderation…"

"You're kidding. The FDA would insist Imortalon be withdrawn if they believed you, which they won't. They don't possess…"

"Quit stalling! Don't possess what?"

A crafty expression crossed his Slavic features "…the subsequent animal studies…"

"*Subsequent?* Later?"

"The short-term ones Martha conducted for me before she became ill. They showed the rodents developed a craving for ARP when they received larger amounts. Their hunger couldn't be assuaged."

"So the rats *were* addicted?"

"Maybe they had PDS—the psychological dependency syndrome."

"Where are those records?"

"I won't reveal a thing unless, one last time, you'll join me in the bedroom."

He was willing to risk exposure of potentially incriminating documents in order to have sex with her? Maybe. But he wouldn't make it easy. "Are you trying to bribe me again?"

"Sure."

Why the hell not? What did she stand to lose that she hadn't already lost? Her pride and dignity, that's what.

On the other hand, she'd slept with him before so it wouldn't be a promiscuous act, only a flirtation and didn't count. Besides, men were promiscuous and a woman could play the same game.

"No," she said weakly.

"No, you say?"

"Yes."

"I'm strong. I could force you."

So she lay there, passive, though the old-young man's vigor, instead of being diminished, had actually increased.

He wasn't going to murder her—not in a rental house, at least. And she assumed, he still took pride in being a person of his word.

Before Mark drove them to the city, she pestered Zig for information.

"Where are those records?"

But Szaba would only hint, as if that fulfilled his side of the bargain. "You've already been there."

"So tell me."

"No."

Where, goddammit? Under his bed at the Carlyle? The office? The factory? Almost any place.

But suppose he'd outsmarted her? Placed himself inside her head and made the same deduction she would?

When she searched for the records he and, oh God, Veere would be there. This time, Szaba would have her killed and she had to resist.

CHAPTER 21

▼

She was beginning to unravel, and, in her apartment again, poured herself a bowl of cereal—eating seemed to calm her—the flow of gastric juices seemed to sooth her nerves. She thought awhile and then contacted Stover. "I have important information."

"Regarding?"

"ARP."

"The Aging Retardant Protein—I remember." He must have sensed from her brevity she didn't want to talk on the phone. "Will your schedule bring you to Washington?"

Schedule? She'd never really had one. "I'll try."

"When?"

"Soon perhaps."

"Will you be free for dinner?"

"I'll do my best."

"Oh," he finally said, "I read in today's Wall Street Journal you've been appointed president of Imortalex. Congratulations."

"Thanks."

She hung up, surprised that Szaba had come through with the offer and without telling her. Sure, she'd attract media attention, which would publicize the product and, to him, she'd be easy to restrain, being just a kid. Maybe, as far as he was concerned, she would not object too hard to commercial irregularities.

Like the addicted rodents.

Columbia wouldn't let her recreate the experiment for any number of reasons: Carlos' still-unsolved murder, the altercation with the veep, the failure to pay royalties, etc. They'd refuse to give her rats from the Animal Storage Unit and the anti-aging protein wouldn't be shipped from the factory. So she'd be unable to prove the rats had become addicted.

Which left the records. At the factory? Yes, she'd been there before but perhaps, in her haste, had overlooked Martha's observations on the rodents.

What about the addiction problem? Should she call the police, the FBI, the DEA, an alphabet soup of letters? Nobody would believe her; they think she'd flipped out. And Szaba would have ample grounds to dismiss her.

Maybe she deserved a long vacation at her elegant house in New Jersey. It would be nice to converse with her dad and play with the horses. But she'd be watched for the rest of her days if she failed to act and now.

The logical answer had to be in Newark. Perhaps Szaba wouldn't believe she had so much courage.

She required assistance, though. She couldn't break into the heavily-guarded factory alone. But she had no one except Greenberg, whose limp put him at too much risk.

Who else? An emptiness, a void. It served her right for having so few friends. Wait a minute. The human testing...The professional guinea pig...No...The acrobat with the red mustache? Perfect.

At her apartment she found the notebook containing the names, addresses and phone numbers of the subjects. Lester Buford. Like her, he lived on the upper West Side, home to moderate to low-income people.

She remained in her four-story walk-up because her days in New York were numbered. Soon, she'd again be a New Jerseyite.

Buford didn't live far from her. She phoned.

"Who?"

"Freddie Ferguson," she repeated.

"Oh yes. The test lady."

"And you're the acrobat."

"High wire man, actually."

"Something I'd like to discuss. Could we meet?"

"Is this another test?"

"But not the same kind of test. This one's more challenging."

Maybe challenges appealed to the high-wire guy. He'd been arrested for a break-in...

They arranged to meet in Riverside Park in an hour.

*   *   *   *

The flame-colored mustache sat next to her on a bench. Long red hair dangled over his raincoat collar—spring showers were expected. She tried to take his measure from his face. The chin seemed a bit weak but the blue eyes were bold. Of course, physiognomy meant nothing. Next to nothing. No, nothing.

The eye and hair color, the shape of the chin, were inherited characteristics. Like the size of breasts and reproductive organs. Admit it, you liked Zig's. But not the rest of him. *He is insane.*

She asked Buford if he enjoyed risks.

"Risks?"

"You know, risking your life."

Oh well, that's what he lay on the line as a performer. At the top of a tent with only a rod for balance.

"But what if you lacked a safety net?"

He never looked down. He weren't no scaredy cat. What did she want him for?

"To get into a building from across the street."

"A robbery?"

"Of course not. Well, not exactly."

"Am I paid for this?"

The same as before. Five hundred bucks.

"One night?"

"Yes."

"When?"

Tomorrow. She looked at him with a steady gaze.

Good. His wife played bridge on Tuesdays. Somebody tended to the kids.

He told her what he needed.

*   *   *   *

Freddie spent the rest of the night with a legal pad. She wrote a will, leaving the house, the land, the horses, the Imortalex stock she still possessed, to her dad. She bequeathed the cash in the bank to Greenberg—dear Noah, he undoubtedly hadn't found a job and was too proud to phone. Her body went to medical science for research. Oh God.

As a bitter-sweet joke, Szaba would inherit her Mad Av clothes—he could give them to Iris Dove!

Early, she ran to Broadway to find a Notary Public.

Next she wrote a detailed note to herself on the factory, including diagrams of what she recalled. She remembered a spiral staircase leading down from the roof.

But where were the animal records? A vital question, *the* vital question. If she failed to find the documents, Imortalon would flood the market and she'd resign, effective immediately.

She'd have to resign in any event.

She spent the morning at the office clearing out her desk—Zig was supposed to be on a business trip. In the afternoon she went to a hardware store to buy thin rope, sturdy wire, flashlights....

She fetched Buford in her car and they drove wordlessly through the Holland Tunnel and into New Jersey. Approaching Newark, he finally asked, "Why are we in black?"

He wore a black leotard and tights as she'd suggested. She had them on too, under her topcoat. "So as not to be seen."

"Oh."

"Yeah. Obviously."

It was dark on the block with the street light out though the factory's small glass windows glowed from interior illumination. She told him what to do; carrying the wire and rope around your neck, shimmy up the side of the building; leave the rope (which by now had knots tied in it), fasten the wire and drop it; climb down, holding the wire; climb up the wall of the rooming house across the street (hardly anyone's there, it seems), with your balancing rod; fasten the wire securely; cross the narrow street on the wire; drop the rope and pull me up. I don't weigh much.

Whew! She'd said it. Actually succeeded in making her plan clear with lots of "ups and downs", the plainest words in the language. She watched him clamber up the factory wall and drop the wire from the roof. He descended to the street, climbed the opposite wall, secured the wire, and with his balancing staff, walked above the street, gracefully.

If he fell, she'd most likely have to call an ambulance and that would be that. She couldn't just leave him with a broken leg or worse. The siren would alert the factory and the president of Imortalex and her henchman would be charged with attempted robbery. How bizarre!

But not as bizarre as a drug on the market having the opposite effect from the intended one.

She and the hero above on the wire had to succeed.

The knotted rope came down and he dragged her up and now she stood with him on the roof. The factory was the largest building on this side of the street. There was no other way to get there except by parachute or helicopter. She located the door that led below, was secured by nothing more than a simple lock—she managed to pick with a sharp tool she'd bought at the hardware store and carried it in a small shoulder bag.

The door ajar, they stood on a small landing from which a spiral staircase led below. "Here goes," she told Buford, and he followed her down the stairs.

They quickly reached the level that contained the vat in which the protein was "cooked". Siphons removed the top layer, the monkey virus, a clear liquid, went into stoppered vials, which, when cooled, were stored by hand in the freezer. She thought of Szaba. It wouldn't take much to steal the virus.

The bottom of the vat formed an inverted pyramid from which the compound was extracted and placed in capsules which dropped into the jars on the loading platform and shipped to pharmacies. Yes, that was where she'd escape, if necessary.

They climbed down into what had been the foyer but which had become a meeting room. A notice on the table advised of a two-day biotech conference in Baltimore. That must be where Zig had gone.

But she had to put her mind on the animal records. There *had* they gone? She hadn't much time—nobody in the guardroom seemed to have noticed them but soon they almost certainly would.

The lights were on and she could see the opening in the ceiling that led to the dead storage area. Was that the place to look? Even if Szaba was playing a weird game of entrapment, he wouldn't expect she'd repeat herself. She was more intelligent than that.

Okay, where? If the rodents had become addicted it wasn't because of the protein; it had to have been the virus that threw them out of whack. Zig was a joke, partly because of his European pseudocharm. Suddenly she knew he'd put the records near the virus. A dare!

She pointed silently and the high-wire man remounted the stairs with her. She opened the unlocked freezer door. She'd deduced properly. Manila folders were sandwiched between the vials.

She told Buford to leave via the roof and the rope. He'd already been paid. She threw him keys and told him to take the car home. She'd come for it on the train.

Inside the folders were studies not previously seen by her. And memos in Martha's handwriting, with conclusions.

Dear Prof. Mulheran:

I have been checking the food intake of the test rodents. It is as though they have a craving for the protein. I've tried feeding them standard chow but they won't touch it, from which I judge they've ingested sufficient food. But then I give them the protein and suddenly they're hungry again.

M.B.

Dear Prof. Mulheran:

The control rats spurn the protein, I guess they're not used to the substance. It's a little like heroin; if you haven't tried the stuff, you don't want it.

M.B.

P.S. As per your instructions, I haven't told Fredericka as you call her. PPS. I love you.

So! Geoff and Martha had been in collusion. Him, because he hoped to make a fortune off the drug, she because she desperately wanted to gain his favor. And Mulheran had sent the memos to Szaba who had concealed the facts from Freddie, as had Geoff and Martha.

Wait a minute. The anti-aging drug didn't contain a narcotic and couldn't be addictive in the usual sense. It must be a psychological effect, as Szaba said. The subject rats wanted more, as though they guessed or intuited, the protein was a source of well-being. Was that theory impossible? She didn't think so.

The same would apply to people. ARP made you feel young and vibrant until age finally caught up.

She visualized a gray new world with old people who considered themselves youthful because of Imortalon. They'd kick up their heels, have a ball, until the monkey virus gave them awful headaches and they suddenly aged—you'd have to take more protein to regain your youth but you'd only have greater headaches. How much protein would you need? An endless cycle…

Oh brave gray new world…Nature exacts a price, side effects…

She gradually became aware of another presence in the room—Szaba, pointing a stungun at her.

"Were they a good read?"

"What?"

"Martha's memos. Spellbinding, I suppose."

"She never struck me as especially imaginative."

"Well, in fact, she was. Those were her love letters to Mulheran, designed to attract his attention."

"Mash notes, huh? Without a shred of truth?"

"None."

"Addicts always deny their habit. Maybe the compound's addictive in some other way. As cigarettes are. You've taken plenty of the stuff and ought to know."

His knuckles turned white. Was it from pressure on the trigger or had he begun to fall apart? She had to get out of there.

"I like you in a leotard," he murmured. "The black contrasts nicely with your blond hair and you're all curves. Exceptional!"

"Like the sauce at The Plaza, I suppose."

"Mmmmm."

There was no doubt in her mind what he wanted but she'd rather have died than give in. She eyed the floor where a tank went down to a capsule machine. Just enough room to squeeze through.

He fondled the butt of the stun gun. An electric cord trailed behind, leading to the guardroom where the DC plug was. "It won't hurt," Szaba said. "You'll feel a shock and fall unconscious. After that, well…"

Veere entered with a syringe. A globule dangled from the needle. He'd jab her and she'd contract a fatal disease. After she was incoherent, with a high fever, she'd be left at a hospital to die. The perfect crime.

Like Martha's murder.

"Give me the folders, Freddie," Szaba said, voice resigned.

"And you won't stun me?"

"You have my word."

"Or inject me?"

She'd never felt this helpless.

"If you'll promise not to talk to the FDA."

"You'd let me go?"

Zig glanced at Veere. "Agreed."

She clutched the folders to her bosom as if they could shield her from the gun or the needle. All the while she'd been edging closer to the tank.

Szaba raised the gun and idly sprayed the wall with electricity. Veere moved closer with the syringe.

She reached out and touched the tank as though for protection.

Zig was saying, "Easy, girl. Don't test us. You haven't met my terms. But I don't want to lose you. You have a highly-paid position. You own stock in our company. The world is yours and so am I. You only have to accept my terms…"

"Okay."

"Okay, what?" he shouted.

"Okay, okay."

"*Okay, okay, what?*" he whined, sounding old and irascible.

Freddie had to tweak him before she disappeared. "You want to live forever like this? A despicable old man haunted by memories of me? A babe you murdered?"

"What care I?" he yelled, screwing up the grammar. He touched the trigger. Soon she'd be dead with no witnesses except Veere. Why'd didn't he just stun her and get it over with? Freddie had a sudden apercu. He still needs me to promote the stock.

Szaba lowered the gun and she slid down the tank, landing on the encapsulator, scrambling across it and dropping to the loading platform next to a fork lift. Clambering over boxes of Imortalon, she pressed a red button and the steel door raised. There were steps to the street. In the darkness she ran to the railroad station, thinking of the joke about a terminal illness. It wasn't funny now.

CHAPTER 22

▼

Freddie boarded the next Amtrak train from Newark to Washington but got off in Baltimore, having paid for the ride with money from her shoulder bag, in which she'd stuffed her topcoat.

She'd remembered the biotech conference; she ought to attend one while she was still in the business; tomorrow she'd leave the scene forever.

What if she ran into Szaba? He couldn't be back in Baltimore. Yet.

She covered the leotard with the topcoat and grabbed a taxi at the Baltimore railroad depot, asking the driver to take her to a modestly-priced hotel near the waterfront.

It was much too late to reach Ted Stover at the FDA but she had the card with his home number. The answering machine picked up and she said she'd call tomorrow. Exhausted, she went to sleep.

Sweet dreams? Yeah, sure. Tossing on her bed, she had the worst nightmares, of rats being guillotined and Martha, of Prof Mulheran and Carlos. Three murders. All had been sacrificed on the altar of Imortalon. And she wasn't safe yet, her dreams told her. First thing in the morning, she left the hotel.

Biotechnology was a multi-billion dollar business and she couldn't afford to look cheap. The harbor, the pride of the city, had fancy stores—Mad Av clones—and she bought a chic outfit: a sailor suit with bell-bottomed trousers, silk shirt. The jacket had ivory buttons and wide lapels. In spike heels, though a bit wobbly, she was over six feet tall and imposing. She no longer wanted obscurity but to attract attention. The world must learn the magic protein could endanger health and sanity. Perhaps there should be a notice on the jars—

SURGEON GENERAL'S WARNING
IMORTALON CONTAINS MONKEY VIRUS

What better place to spread the word than in an assemblage of leading pharmaceutical and biotech firms. They'd be alert to biohazards.

She checked in at the registration table by the entrance: "Are you on the list?"

She wanted to say yes but "no" came out.

"Why are you here then?"

"Because I want to be."

"You received an invitation?"

"The company did."

"What company?"

"Imortalex, miss."

"You're employed by Imortalex?"

"Yes, miss, I'm the president."

"You are, are you? Are you? You *are*. Fredericka…"

"Ferguson," a man added.

Imortalon had made Imortalex famous and so was she. They typed her name on a badge and she went in.

The well-dressed crowd was festive. People drank at the cash bar though it was before noon. A woman eyed her badge, "You're rich like the rest of us."

"Am I?" The woman was gauche but Freddie didn't mean to be timid.

"Got to be. The price of your stock…."

"Don't bank on it."

"….is through the roof, exceeding expectations. Like most biotech companies. We're discovering cures for most everything that ails us."

"Except death, maybe."

"And you have a remedy for that."

A scholarly-looking man with a bump on his head and a pince-nez interjected, "You're about to bring us postmortal society."

"Postmortal?" Freddie asked.

"Because of your new drug people will have life-spans of two hundred, I read."

"At least," she murmured.

"Have you considered the demographic implications? Take Italy. The Italians suffer from a *bambini* bust—the lowest fertility rate in the world. 1.2 kids per woman, in some places less than that. The replacement rate, just to maintain the population, is 1.6. So Italy's population will shrink from its current level, about 57 million, to 41 million in the next 50 years."

"Ample time to adjust," the woman said.

"Is it? Every year you'll have fewer and fewer wops. The same is true for the rest of Europe, which will lose 15 percent of the population. Probably couldn't even fight a war."

"Hooray," Freddie said.

"But that's not the dark—gray, I mean—side. Thanks to global aging, old people will dominate the world. The age boomers. In the next few years, the over-65 crowd in Italy will account for 20 percent of the population. With Japan and the U.S not far behind. Think of that! Old-old people outnumbering the very young! It's unprecedented and alarming. Who's to pay the oldsters' medical bills with the cost of nursing care constantly rising? And with the percent of younger workers heading down? Many countries will have to raise taxes or go broke because of greater longevity."

She understood all too well. The conclusion was self-evident; Mulheran had already reached it. Imortalon would accelerate a tragic trend toward a postmortal society. As she projected the outcome, half the people would be in nursing homes and the other half taking care of them.

With graybeards at the helm, setting the tone, undoubtedly conservative, without much flair—ooompf—would life be worth living?

What kind of clothes would Calvin Klein or Tommy Hilfiger design when they'd reached 100? What sort of films would come from centenarian Steven Spielberg?

But didn't medicine and biotechnology have the same objective as Imortalon?

The man in the pince-nez pulled at Freddie's sleeve. He worked for a biotech company, according to his badge. "We're different from you. We seek to create freedom?"

"From?"

"The discomfort of illness."

"Isn't that tantamount to living longer in good health?"

"A byproduct," he assured her.

Really? Everyone here is dedicated to the conquest of disease. At this rate, nobody will be sick. And they're certainly not suggesting we'll have shorter life spans.

But *she* might. She spotted Iris Dove at the Imortalex booth.

Freddie said to the biotech man, "It's a conundrum. You want to provide perfect health but you won't accept the evil consequences of global aging. You're a bunch of hypocrites."

"No," he answered. "We never dreamed of promoting eternal bliss, as the Imortalon literature implies. Still, there might be a catch."

"Oh?"

"I just saw the TV news. They're constantly repeating the broadcast. Luckily for you, it's only on a local station. He led her behind the bar and she saw a repeat of the news flash. The anchor said, "We go once more to a Baltimore suburb."

The cameras showed a sign: IMORTALEX COMMUNE. PRIVATE. KEEP OUT.

A steel fence topped by concertina wire had a metal gate and it was open.

The reporter's voice was hard to hear above the din from the conference crowd but Freddie listened with interest that turned to awe. "Something transpired," he means happened, Freddie thought, "here this morning. The police noted a small group of people wandering on the street. We asked one how old he was, assuming he'd be at least 90."

The camera showed a man bent over nearly double, supporting himself with a cane. He looked up and whispered, "I'm 65."

"You can't be telling the truth, sir."

"I am. It transpired almost overnight. I can't stand up straight and my hair fell out. My teeth too." His rueful grin revealed just gums. "I had lots of sex but who wants to make love to a woman who *was* attractive but now looks like she's ready for the grave?"

"Are all of you in the same condition?"

"Yeah, pretty much. We got old all at once."

"Does that about sum it up?"

"No. We have splitting headaches."

"As if you have a disease?"

"Uh-huh. I'm a former physician and I'd have to guess a communicable one like the…"

The oldster faltered and then went on, "My mind is going too."

"You were about to make a comparison. Like the…?"

"Plague."

The reporter said hurriedly, "Health authorities here have quarantined the members of the Imortalex community. This Baltimore suburb has the jitters, fearing an epidemic of extreme old age."

The biotech man murmured, "So much for adding extra years to your life."

The reporter was saying, "Did any of you suddenly die?"

"No. Our health seems fine. Although much older, we could last I think, possibly forever, unless we kill each other."

"So there you have it," the reporter announced. "An outbreak of immediate aging, accompanied severe headaches. The authorities remain puzzled by the question of who or what to blame for what might have been a disaster."

Freddie knew—overdoses of the magic protein. Fuck! Wasn't that Szaba in a camelhair jacket edging through the crowd toward Iris? And Freddie recognized the flashy couple she'd met in Paris. The Polish mafia…

Best to get out of here. Hurry!

She had started to run in her high heels when Zig intercepted her. "Freddie!" he clamored, as if nothing had happened. "We're the hit of the biotech conference. Aren't you pleased? Imortalon's already the rage. I have a hospitality suite at the Hyatt. Won't you join us?"

She had to hide. But before that she had to act normal. "Sure. Why don't I meet you there?"

"Len Veere will bring you in the Daimler."

"Okay. Where's the car?"

"Parked in front."

"I have to pee."

Zig grinned. "That's *sikac* in Polish."

She'd seen the sign for the women's room and scampered in that direction. Iris, displaying creamy breastwork, purred into a mike, as pictures of a baby with a man's face flashed on a screen, "Enjoy everlasting youth with Imortalon."

"Bullshit," Freddie snapped as she passed by.

Iris put down the mike, seized Freddie's arm, tried, unsuccessfully, to kiss her, and said, "We'll make a *killing* with Imortalon."

"Yeah," Freddie said, thinking of the news broadcast which obviously the Imortalon bunch hadn't seen.

She found the ladies' john but continued to walk to the exit. She removed the towering heels, placing them under her arm and slid from the door.

Two guys in narrow-brimmed hats stood there smoking unfiltered cigarettes—Poles, of course—looked at her as she ambled down the street, put on the shoes and kept walking.

A mistake, she decided, when she saw the limousine, Mark at the wheel, heading toward her.

She watched herself, as though from outside, a tall, blond woman who ripped of the heels from her shoes and ran like crazy on the flat soles.

She was thinking only of escape in a strange city from a strange and desperate man.

Somewhere she'd read Edgar Allen Poe was buried in Baltimore. He would have understood my terror.

I am sweating red corpuscles through my pores. The blood will get into my eyes, blind me. I wipe my forehead. It's just sweat. The blood is imaginary. So maybe is escape.

To my right the way is blocked by a superhighway, US.95, the sign says. A big hotel stands to my left. Across is what seems to be a housing project. I'll run through it.

The limo can't pass.

She reaches Conway Street and spots the harbor. All roads in downtown Baltimore lead to the waterfront. I won't be hard to find but I have no choice.

What then? Szaba will be in hot pursuit. Maybe she'll have to swim, make like one of the crabs Baltimore is famous for.

She catches sight of the Daimler with other cars behind. Must be the Poles. They're coming down Light Street in both directions. *I'm trapped. Veere will subdue me with that awful needle.*

I want to scream.

Suddenly she spots a blue boat with "Water Taxi" printed on the side about to leave the dock. Tourists pack the boat. How does she know they're tourists? Because they're fat. Can the taxi take another passenger? Always room for one more, it seems. Maybe the boat will capsize from the weight and she'll have to swim after all.

Freddie leaps on to the deck. Her fancy sailor suit amuses the passengers who are plainly dressed, but not Szaba, who is too late to stop her. A horn toots and the boat enters the harbor, powered by outboard motors.

Freddie watches a chain gang in blue uniforms jog past, chanting. They're not prisoners, she realizes, but Baltimore cops, training. If only they'd rescue her from Szaba who's checking what seems to be the schedule posted on the pier. He'll have little or no trouble finding her. *Unless, that is, I get to the taxi's destination first.*

Almost by instinct, she leaves the boat at Fells Point.

No Szaba. He and his cronies haven't arrived yet, maybe got lost in Baltimore though it seems to be a simple and straightforward city.

Freddie pauses to reconnoiter. The square at Fells Point has a hotel, more like an inn, with everything painted and polished. Too fancy to be anonymous in. The streets around it are filled with rundown stores, some of which sell what look like cruddy antiques, period-piece jewelry and costumes and food. *I don't believe I've ever seen so many restaurants and bars in a small area. I've a hunch it's a great place for alcoholics. Mulheran would fit right in here.*

On a pay phone she calls Stover but he isn't expected back in his office until morning, so she decides to spend a night here before trying to get to Washington. A mistake?

She walks across the square filled with children and down Thames Street where she finds a bed and breakfast place with just two rooms. They won't accept credit cards, and Freddie has very little cash on her. She didn't bring checks. She pays in advance and sits by the window, staring out at a big brick building that must have been an armory. Weren't American cities like armed camps once? Didn't they fear uprisings and revolts? Slave rebellions? Food riots?

She half expected to see the Daimler on Thames Street but that's impossible. Zig has no way to locate her.

It's started to rain, which makes Freddie depressed. She toys with the idea of suicide, but Noah's lean face—a nice face, actually—intervenes. He has courage and she must too. If he can live with Pompe's disease, she can survive in Baltimore.

Freddie remembers reading once that suicide is a girl thing. *Well, I ain't that sort of girl. My dad didn't bring me up to kill myself.*

Anyhow, she has a mission: to get Imortalon off the market. *I must show Stover the latest rodent reports. He'll flip. Adverse findings....*

$$*\qquad*\qquad*\qquad*$$

Freddie may have been tough but she had appetite to contend with. Her stomach was an empty hole that yawned to be filled.

With what? Toilet tissue? Except for a canapé she'd nibbled at the conference, she hadn't eaten since fuck knew when. Frantic, she yearned for nourishment.

Okay. She'd leave the bed and breakfast. The car on the street had parking lights on; was it Zig's? Hard to tell in the downpour.

She borrowed an umbrella from the b&b proprietor. Rain rat-tatted on the nylon surface as she emerged. She scurried to the corner where she'd seen a fish joint. The prices were absurdly cheap.

She was enjoying her meal until Szaba appeared and sat across from her.

"Zig!" she gasped.

"You're wondering how I found you?" he said with a bright-toothed smile. "I figured you'd leave the water taxi at Fells Point because you'd be harder to locate.

But the good people here notice everything, especially a beautiful woman in a sailor suit. A standout! They told me where to find you and I did."

"Oh."

"What are your plans, Freddie?"

"Aside from avoiding execution? I made myself clear…"

"To go to the FDA with an incredible story? Something you made up to get back at the company, eh?"

"Why would I?"

"Because you were fired. Or, rather, allowed to quit. I have your letter of resignation on my desk."

"I wrote no such letter," she protested.

"You dictated one to your secretary. She'll swear to that, in court if necessary."

"She will? Was she tortured?"

"Yes. By you. You subjected her to verbal abuse—the profanity—and you resigned rather than face a harassment suit."

"Next thing you'll be accusing me of is that I'm a lesbian."

"Not a bad idea. That's what the lawyers suggested, as a matter of fact."

"I could kill you, Zig."

"Maybe you'll have to. I wonder what the penalty is for murdering a man who has at least double the normal life expectancy. Two lethal injections? Twice as many volts?" He smirked.

"Listen. I intend to talk to the government and nothing can stop me."

"I wouldn't be so sure, were I you. I have Polish mafiosi guarding the bus and railroad depots."

"I'll take a cab to Washington."

"Have you the fare?" he seemed to taunt.

"Of course."

"In your hotel room? You left the shoulder bag with the money on the bed and the dough is not there any more."

Either Mark or he must have picked the flimsy lock. She would have stored the cash at the desk but there hadn't been much and now there was none to pay a taxi with. Thank God she'd paid the bed and breakfast in advance.

For one night. She *had* to depart Baltimore.

She could have induced her dad to wire money but didn't know where he was in Atlantic City. And Noah seemed to have vanished.

She had to survive the night.

She let Szaba pay for her fish sandwich.

"This is my last warning. Stay away from the government."

"Yeah? Screw you."

"You're a remarkable pretty girl, Freddie. To have heavy scars on your face would be a crying shame."

"Who would cut me?"

"Veere."

"So I would be found in the harbor?"

"Like Martha in a sense. After that the forensic guys would saw your skull open."

*   *   *   *

The dialogue was imaginary, in her head. But his dark eyes, filled with hatred, said it all. She'd merely supplied the rejoinders.

Szaba left.

She was afraid to return to her room. She had to hide for the rest of the night.

She wandered the waterfront, disconsolate. The rain had ceased and after awhile the moon came out, a pale orb, fringed with wispy white clouds, as if the moon had suddenly aged. So had she, Freddie felt. Shoulders back, straighten up. Don't slump. Ignore the fatigue. Stay alert, vigilant.

She sat on a bench.

Dawn finally broke with bewildering speed—she must have nodded off—and a cop stood near the bench uncertainly. His blue uniform was rumpled as though from extensive walking. He carried a nightstick and had been ready to poke her.

"Are you homeless?"

"No, sir."

"Are you soliciting?"

Was she a whore? He meant. "No."

"Do you need medical attention?" Was she schizo or something?

"I'm very much all right. Thank you."

"Do you have a place to stay?"

She gave him the name of the bed-and-breakfast. An inn, she called it.

The cop looked at her as if to reassure himself she was just a young woman who rose early and he sauntered off. The sun was up. They'd be waiting for her at the B&B but she wouldn't go there. From a public phone she dialed Stover but his answering machine responded again.

How to get to D.C.?

Not far from Fells Point she'd seen a neighborhood called Little Italy which seemed to specialize in food. She found a truck headed for Washington with a load of squid and hitched a ride. She asked the driver to drop her in the vicinity of Chevy Chase where Stover lived, she knew from his card. She trotted to his house and, on the warm front porch, promptly went to sleep.

*   *   *   *

Freddie woke in darkness, confused as to where she was. Perhaps in Short Hills, where she longed to be, perhaps in Szaba's castle, a nightmare, which meant Zig had somehow spirited her away. She'd languish in the crypt with Mark checking the chains that bound her, and Veere injecting her with massive amounts of protein. Soon she'd have a terrible headache; in fact she already had one.

A shadow....Stover!

"Out of town when I got your message...rushed back."

The FDA man must have been sensitive to the anxiety in her voice. Now she said, I'm glad you did, I have something to show you."

"Come inside. Calm down. I'll fix us dinner."

He had a chicken pot pie in the freezer and after they'd eaten and drunk some wine she felt better. The headache evaporated. Must have been hunger and nerves.

"ARP-1," she began.

"I don't discuss business at home and never at night. Can't you come to the office tomorrow?"

"No. I'm going home."

"New York?"

"New Jersey. Could you be a friend and lend me a hundred bucks?" In addition to a ticket she'd need cab fare to Short Hills.

Ted's beard smiled affectionately from his beard. "I reckon. What brings you to our nation's capital?"

"Imortalon."

"Why, for God's sake? The drug's been certified."

"An error. A gross error."

"Go on."

"Well, the stuff seems beneficial—it counters the aging process, you don't grow old—but there's a side effect."

"Nothing like that appeared in the human studies."

"No." Martha's case had been suppressed. "The stuff is habit-forming if you take too much. I have proof. The rodents."

"Show me."

She dug into the pockets of the wide-lapelled jacket and handed him the pages. His brow furrowed as he read. "Why haven't I seen these before?"

"Imortalex didn't want you to know. It's nobody's fault but mine. And ARP will lead to violent headaches and a pandemic of communicable old age. Haven't you heard the news about a Baltimore suburb?"

"No. I avoid TV. I haven't read today's papers though I listened to the other news on the car radio. It startled me."

"I haven't the slightest idea what you're talking about."

"The President, backed by the Joint Chiefs of Staff, wants a missile defense system that will protect us from the entire world, including Canada and Mexico, our neighbors who don't possess missiles. It's as if the government has lost touch with reality."

Freddie remembered she'd sent Imortalon kits to Washington. The officials must have taken the capsules. The protein must have conferred grandiose visions, like Zig's.

"Temporary insanity. A diplomatic embarrassment is all. I wish the same applied to the headaches. Because of them, I quit my job at the company."

"I didn't know."

"You shall, Theodore." The news would be all over the financial media.

He said decisively, "We'll have to issue a notice of adverse findings. Imortalon must be withdrawn from the market."

Just in time, too, because America would have been filled with fiends like Szaba, and places like the Baltimore suburb where they'd experienced the "Shangri-la" effect, as she termed it—you stopped taking the capsules and mysteriously aged. The factory would be shut down; maybe Zig would find another occupation and quit trying to see her.

Ted drove Freddie to the station to catch a night train. There was no sign of Zig or his henchmen. "By the way," she said, "could the FDA use an experienced chemist?"

"Depends."

She told him of Greenberg.

"Is he your boyfriend?"

"Not in the least."

"In that case have him call me. Shall we meet again?"

She kissed him dispassionately. "Why not? In Short Hills."

Much could happen there.

PART IV

▼

THE FIEND

CHAPTER 23

▼

Behind the house, the lawn and gunnite swimming pool with its jaunty parasols, white plastic railings outlined her acreage on which the horses were free to graze and roam. The fence stopped before her father's cottage and when she saw his old, polished Cadillac there she strolled across the field.

Frederick no longer bothered with a phone. The line was expensive and he mostly lived in Atlantic City.

"How are things at the poker table?"

"I'm still a rock."

"You must be gambling all time."

"I often take morning walks on the boardwalk when it's not too hot."

"This summer's been miserable. So when do you play poker?"

"Usually in the late afternoons."

"What about evenings?"

"I...have a companion."

Startled, Freddie said, "A woman?"

"Who else, for God's sake? She rather resembles your mother, I'm ashamed to admit."

"Ashamed?"

"Well, you know, I swore to be faithful to my wife's memory."

"Mother wouldn't object. She's dead."

"Not to me, daughter. I feel as though I'm being unfaithful."

"Grounds for divorce, huh?" she said sarcastically.

"You've become hard, Freddie?"

"And you're morbid, Dad. Enjoy the woman."

"I intend to, especially because I'm winning a little at poker. Life is good if you limit your goals," he said.

"I try. I don't want much."

"Just a mansion and a horse farm, eh? How are the equines?"

"Magnificent, especially the one you gave that special feed to. They never seem to age."

"As I remember, one of them died, however."

"Nothing's perfect. And they removed the protein from the market."

"Why?"

"Habit-forming and potentially dangerous."

"Like you, huh?" He smiled. "Well, it appears to me you're off the market too, Freddie. You've been holed up here for days now. Are you preparing for nun-hood?"

*   *   *   *

She might as well have been.

She hadn't planned to become a recluse but that was how it had worked out. There was no one she felt an urgent need to see and she preferred to read poetry like Joyce Kilmer's "Trees".

"I think that I shall never see or, a poem lovely as a tree." More to her moods, William Cullen Bryant's "Thanatopsis."

> "When thoughts
> Of the last bitter hour come like a blight
> Over thy spirit, and sad images
> And breathless darkness, and the narrow house,
> Make thee to shudder, and grow sick at heart."

And tend to the horses. She'd been training them and they galloped over when she whistled, receiving cubes of brown sugar as a reward.

Stover arrived for a visit but somehow the relationship failed to work.

She asked herself the reason. Stover, a bureaucrat, expected things to be regulated. She was too unpredictable to be standardized. She couldn't guarantee a steady output or uniformity. He wouldn't like her frequent mood swings. She was just too, well, hormonal and shouldn't ask him to put up with her even if he wanted to, which he might. At least he said so but her instincts provided contrary information.

Ted told her Greenberg had applied for a job, as Freddie had suggested.

Noah got a job with the FDA's New York office and was overjoyed though she refused to accept his gratitude. "You did it on your own," she told him on the telephone.

"Without you I'd be nothing."

"Untrue. You persevere, Noah. That's what counts."

"That's what the Prof would have said. I still want to bring you a present."

"Wait until I need one."

She feared he'd be in a wheelchair, the last thing she wished to witness, hating pity.

She occupied her time methodically, with the horses, reading scientific journals and occasionally taking target practice in the barn with a .22. She wasn't certain why except the pistol made her feel comfortable when she thought of Szaba.

She resisted Zig's entreaties.

*   *   *   *

Since she was without a mortgage or any other kind of debt, Freddie had sufficient cash to survive (barely) from the sale of most of her Imortalex shares. The corporation was bankrupt, she thought, but suddenly she received a small dividend check.

Why?

Once in awhile she watched TV and saw an ad for Migranex, outselling Advil, Tylenol, Excedrin, Bayer and all the rest. At a drugstore where she bought some Migranex she discovered it was manufactured by Imortalex in New Jersey and described as a herbal cure. Meant to improve memory, it also was supposed to alleviate headaches which were spreading like the flu.

So Szaba had bypassed the FDA. By the time the government caught up with Migranex (if it did) Zig would be a billionaire.

Instinctively, she understood what had happened and, in a fiery rage, called Szaba at the Carlyle.

"You caused the so-called headache epidemic, right?" she screamed. "Aging could have become an epidemic as well."

"Are you using a tape recorder?"

"If only I were. I don't have one," she confessed.

"Then you won't have proof."

"Maybe not but I'm cognizant of what must have occurred. You stole the monkey virus from the factory and somehow spread it around. Your Polish terrorist friends contaminated reservoirs, I bet."

"Oh?"

"And that's not all. You'd already developed a retrovirus..."

"Retrovirus?"

"Don't feign ignorance. It combats the virus. Only you, me and Greenberg understand the composition of the monkey virus, with the prof dead. So you drenched some herbs with the retrovirus and came up with effective relief. It won't last long."

"Migranex improves memory," he insisted.

"Memory of the headaches, right?"

"Right." Zig seemed irritated. "Ms. Ferguson, may I pay you a visit?"

"You don't know where I live."

"Easy to learn."

"When?"

"An hour."

He'd arrive even if she told him not to. The police might come but then they'd go. Szaba would return.

"All right."

She wondered whether she'd have the guts to kill Zig.

She dialed frantically. "Noah, I need you now."

Freddie was tired of being alone.

CHAPTER 24

▼

She removed the .22 from a drawer to be certain it was fully loaded. If he set foot in the house, she'd shoot Szaba and then point the pistol at herself and squeeze the trigger.

She prowled the mansion, lonely for the first time since she'd lived there. The loneliness was like a dreadful ache deep within her body, and nothing in a medicine cabinet would cause it to disappear. The only remedy would be another human's touch.

She stood before the bathroom mirror and inspected her cheek. Under duress, the ugly, fishlike scales of ichthyosis were coming back and she didn't have Rejuvenon. Maybe she didn't give a damn. You had to be pretty for someone, not just for yourself.

She refused to succumb to depression. She cheered herself by remembering she'd developed a skin cream and found a cure for progeria. Not bad for one little life, soon to be over perhaps.

What if I murder Szaba? Could I plead self-defense? Zig would have to fire first but could I wait? My hatred is overwhelming.

Suppose I succeed in killing him? Maybe I could plea bargain for manslaughter. Five or ten years in jail? Lost years. No, I'd be better off as a suicide.

I feel cold already.

The phone rang and she answered. Szaba's voice, from the Daimler, on the cell phone. "Freddie?" He seemed tense.

"Yes?"

"Are you alone?"

"Yes." Goddamit. "Why?"

"Just checking."

He made it sound like a date—for homicide.

She pictured the wavy gray hair, the cruel mouth.

Wait a minute! How could Zig get away with murder? That fucking needle again. She'd be injected with something undetectable and fast-acting. By the time she reached the ER, she'd be a corpse. The autopsy would reveal zilch. Case closed.

She positioned herself in the foyer, gripping the pistol, safety catch off.

The door opened on the driveway. Behind it the fence and the field with the horses.

The silver Daimler crunched slowly over the gravel. The porch light revealed Mark at the wheel, Veere in the back with Szaba who didn't dream she'd shoot.

But I will. Both wrists up like a cop aiming a .45 for accuracy, elbows bent to absorb the shock. The .22 can be a lethal weapon in the right hands.

I'm concentrating on the barrel. Does it waver? If so, I must drop to my knees to aim.

Her hands trembled so she lowered to her knees, clutching the .22.

Veere climbed from the limo—it was like a deadly pantomime—holding a high-powered rifle compared to which the .22 was a peashooter.

Zig figures I'm prepared to resist. Veere will shoot a round or two at the ceiling, covering me with plaster in hopes I'll come out, arms raised. But I won't. I'll wait for Szaba to show himself.

"Freddie, where are you?" Zig called. He was smooth.

Silence was her answer. She fiddled with the safety catch for relief.

Mark, the chauffeur, held a chain with his long arms.

He's the decoy. Szaba hopes to flush me out like a frightened quail. Then Veere will jump on me. Well, I'm too skinny to be appetizing. I'll stay put, I think.

Sheer bravado. All right, I'm terrified. Maybe I should throw myself on Zig's mercy...

Nuts! I won't surrender. I'd rather die.

Szaba had left the limo, apoplectically impatient, snapping his fingers, face red, knowing his pharmaceutical prosperity would collapse if Freddie were not disposed of. She raised the gun.

Before she could pull the trigger an old station wagon rattled into the driveway and parked between Zig and her. Veere lowered the rifle and Greenberg stepped into the light, as in a B movie. Only he wasn't a knight or a cowboy.

He said to Szaba, "Either you leave this instant or I'll summon the police."

Freddie smiled at the bravado but she had to give Noah credit for guts, especially when she saw how badly he limped.

Szaba could barely conceal contempt. "You think you can frighten me?"

"Yes. Freddie will bring charges against you and I'll testify on her behalf."

"You are threatening us?"

"I...."

She emerged and finished for Noah, "He works for the FDA. Migranex...."

But Szaba seeming startled, stepped backwards, uttered a gurgling sound, slapped a hand to his chest and collapsed on the lawn. Freddie quickly put an ear to his chest, gave him mouth-to-mouth resuscitation, and listened again.

"Is he dead?" Noah questioned.

"Just about. Veere! Call 911."

He raised the cell phone.

Freddie said, as they waited for an ambulance, "Weak hearts run in his family. Not even Imortalon could provide him extra years. In fact, it *caused* him to age."

Flashing lights. The ambulance. The EMS technician examined Szaba and said, "He's gone."

Szaba was carried on a stretcher. Veere went with him. The ambulance departed slowly. There was no further need for haste.

Mark drove off in the Daimler.

✳   ✳   ✳   ✳

Freddie and Noah entered the house.

"Sumptuous," he remarked.

"I built the place." She shook her head as if to clear it. "I can't believe Szaba passed away."

"Died, you mean. We hate euphemisms, remember?"

She laughed. "Right. Putting things as they are. We inflict collateral damage on the truth. I have a question for you. Would you be happy living here?"

"Pardon?" He sounded shocked.

"Move in, goddam it."

"With you?"

"Who else? I'd appreciate the companionship."

"I might be difficult. I shave...."

"...sometimes twice a day. That's not a serious objection. We can have separate bathrooms."

"And I'm Jewish. I always go to synagogue on Saturdays."

"I respect your what do you call them? Yes, traditions."

"And I yours."

She giggled. "I don't have any, really. Unless it's science. I'll play bridge on Saturdays with the women."

"You don't know any women."

"I'll meet some."

"Or how to play bridge."

"I'll read the rules."

"Where is the ring?"

"I keep it next to the pistol. Both are deadly weapons."

"Would you wear it?"

"The gun?"

"What is this, a joke. I meant the ring."

"Okay. I will."

"Will?"

"Marry you."

He seemed downcast. I couldn't marry a *shicksa*."

Freddie burst into tears. Crying felt good. "Don't Jewish women cry?"

"A lot. I suppose marriage isn't entirely out of the question...."

"But you'd have to change. You were rather unpleasant in my apartment...."

"I didn't bring wine. I was selfish. Can you forgive me?"

"I guess so." She clapped a hand to her check. "The rash..."

Noah gently but firmly removed her fingers, then kissed the rash. "It will go away."

"We hope."

"Can you tolerate a cripple?"

She smiled. "Indefinitely. I've been with worse."

"Who? Szaba?"

"Don't be malicious, Greenberg. You know damn well who."

"Were you in love with him?"

"I thought I was for a time," she said.

"How long?"

She sighed. "An instant? Eternity? The half-life of a love can't be quantified."

"You make it sound like fissionable material."

"Not a bad comparison. Except..."

"Except?" he wondered.

"Even genuine love, by its very nature, is always losing intensity, they say."

"And you think it doesn't?" he said.

"I'm a skeptic."

"A skeptic! A Protagorian soulmate."

"Roommates is all. Let's give ourselves a chance, Noah."

"Suppose we're not compatible."

"We shouldn't decide until the facts are in. Scientific method…"

"Won't you be haunted by memories of Szaba?"

"No. He's deceased, right?"

"Uh-huh. But, before I agree to marriage, I want you to sign a pre-nup."

"Stipulating?"

"That you bequeath your worldly goods to my synagogue."

"What's in it for you?"

"I'll receive a big stipend as the rabbi."

"Okay." Freddie thought: I'll outlive him by years.

CHAPTER 25

▼

Weeks passed—fulfilling weeks for Freddie and, she hoped, Noah—and suddenly it was fall. A north wind stirred the leaves.

She waved goodbye to Noah, bound for New York in his battered station wagon. He couldn't afford a better one because of debts he'd incurred while unemployed, which he proudly refused to let her help pay off.

Still, he wished to inherit her house—worth a fortune and her dough. She couldn't feel sorry for him—contempt, perhaps. In her weakest moment.

She wished he'd take the train—the car wasn't reliable and sometimes refused to start but independence, symbolized by the car, was a boy thing and she lacked the gumption to argue. Noah had to be humored—he was disabled. But so what? All men were weak.

Every day she went to the stables to curry and comb the horses before putting them out to pasture. It would be winter soon and they'd need oats.

I remember when Dad fed the equines oats drenched in the magic protein. The mare with a white star on her forehead and the enormous stallion are still with me but they don't seem to enjoy each other. Maybe because they're so old. As with magnets, likes repel. And perhaps there's more to it than that. I'm aware it's called the pathetic fallacy to attribute human thoughts and feelings to animals but maybe something similar to rivalry is involved. They "want" to outlive each other at this point—even though they have arthritis and their eyesight is failing. They'd be better off dead, in my opinion.

Mulheran would be horrified by such unscientific speculations but I'll write them down and keep the notes with my papers, as I have before.

My point is, a sort of aging rivalry exists between the horses.

She watched the mare and the stallion slowly gallop and went inside. She ate lunch and napped—she couldn't be a lady of leisure forever; she'd have to find a teaching job at a university—and suddenly it was afternoon.

She heard tires on gravel and, looking outside, saw the silver Daimler parked there, the chauffeur at the wheel.

She met Mark at the door.

"Where's Mr. Veere?"

"I dunno. The boss stuck him in a jar."

"Good God! Replacement parts?"

Mark blinked.

"You mean Zig killed Veere?"

"Uummmmm."

"But how could he have. Mr. Szaba's moribund."

"Huh?"

"Negative."

She recognized the reedy voice and stared across the yard. Szaba sloped into her vision: he stood by the fence. She thought he hadn't changed till he came closer and she saw his face.

Shit! He's alive when he should be dead. What gives him the right to survive? He's not a deity nor does he resemble one.

The nose might have been fashioned with silly putty and he had jagged scars on his cheeks. One eye drooped. The bandanna around his neck didn't entirely conceal open wounds.

"I'm not in the best of shape," he admitted, sarcastically.

Freddie wanted to regurgitate her lunch. "The plastic surgeon hasn't finished?" she managed.

"Not quite—can't you see? But he will be soon. Meanwhile, I'll get by."

"How?"

"The ticker—is that the word?—in the jar let me down so I used Veere's."

"Incredible. Why are you here?"

"To show I'm immortal."

"With one 'm'."

"No. Two. I will exist virtually forever. I'm a survival artist. I've changed my mind about suicide. Cells will renew themselves because I've conquered the death gene. I was able, in the basement, to alter my DNA and eliminate the instructions for aging. Even if I screwed up a bit, I must sleep a lot: I estimate that a person who sleeps half the time will live to 350 years."

"Is it worth it? Remember Methuselah. 'Who calls that livin'/when no gal'd give in/to no man what's nine hundred years'" She quoted Gershwin.

"I've been advised against excitement which would be bad for my new heart," he said.

"You're making me sick," she said calmly. "You're in violation of medical ethics not to mention the law. Veere's inside you. You murdered him."

From the field a horse whinnied.

"That accusation can't be proved."

"Veere's DNA? From his heart?"

"A prosecutor would refuse to handle the case and a jury wouldn't accept it."

"You must be officially out of the picture, Szaba."

"No." He smiled with blue lips. "Veere gave me a shot of ARP in the ambulance and I left the hospital on his arm. I didn't die."

"You could have fooled me, Zig."

"I'm getting angry," he warned. "Enraged, in fact."

"So? Sticks and stones."

"Listen, Freddie, I'll break your bones."

"You're not strong enough, Szaba," she taunted.

"Oh?" he said coldly polite.

He sauntered back to the fence with obvious confidence. The slats were composed of thick plastic. Behind them the horses watched as he raised an arm and, using the edge of his hand, snapped the plastic.

The horses ran, except for the ancient mare and stallion. They pawed the ground.

Szaba slouched toward Freddie.

"Stop!" she screamed in terror.

But he came on, madness in his eyes, one of which protruded from the socket.

"You're dying," she screamed.

"Never!" he roared.

The stallion and mare stood in the gap in the fence.

Freddie took a last look at Szaba and, praying, placed two fingers in her mouth and whistled shrilly. The horses advanced across the lawn and reared. Szaba tried to wave them off but they trampled him until he was merely flesh and blood.

"Mark," she commanded, "take him away."

The chauffeur scooped up the limp body in his long arms and marched to the Daimler.

And that, she thought, is that.

But, hauntingly, Zig's eyes, wide open, stared at her through the limousine's rear window.

So! After Freddie married Noah and tried to be happy, they would always wonder if Szaba still lived. He would always between them like a shadow. The only way to fight a shadow was to block out the sun and you couldn't do that. When Szaba returned, she'd kill him again for sure.

0-595-29762-5